SIX MONTHS
IN IPSWICH

SIX MONTHS IN IPSWICH

mediacake
books

SIX MONTHS IN IPSWICH
Published by MediaCake Inc. Newburyport MA 01950

Available online at: mediacake.com
Second Edition

Copyright © 2010 Alexander DeLuca
All rights reserved.

ISBN13: 978-0-615-33239-0

1. New England - Fiction. 2. Drug traffic - Fiction 3. Love - Fiction
I. Title. Six Months in Ipswich II. Title

Printed in the United States of America

Without limiting the rights under copyright reserved above, no part of this publication may be reproduced, stored in or introduced into a retrieval system, or transmitted, in any form, or by any means (electronic, mechanical, photocopying, recording, or otherwise), without the prior written permission of both the copyright owner and the above publisher of this book.

PUBLISHERS NOTE

This is a work of fiction. Names, characters, places, and incidents either are the product of the author's imagination or are used fictitiously, and any resemblance to actual persons, living or dead, business establishments, events, or locales is entirely coincidental.

In loving memory of Robert Gilbert, the world's best grandfather.
His short stories and musical spirit planted the seedlings of creativity
that spawned this story.

Inspired by William Shakespeare's *A Midsummer's Night Dream*, albeit very loosely.

Dramatic Concept

A small, picturesque New England town appears to be the image of perfection. Just under the surface, however, there is little else but dysfunctional families, class conflict, and substance abuse. Join the residents of Ipswich as one mysterious individual turns their town upside down in hopes of making it a better place. Some may rise to the occasion or fall to their own self pity, as their issues are brought to light and they are offered a rare chance at a brighter future.

Lead Players

Mary Augustine – eighteen, a young, literature obsessed woman, who attends Ipswich High.

Laura Augustine – forty-two, an alcoholic single mother who pines after the husband who left her.

Tanner Prior – eighteen, a young soccer play at Saint Andrews Academy, secretly an avid painter and quite confused.

Gavin Prior – forty-seven, a single father who has gone aloof after the tragic loss of his brother and wife.

George Rutherford – twenty-seven, a failed film maker back in his hometown, going nowhere fast.

Perran Nemerov – a boyish figure that seems to slip into the cracks of everyone's life in one way or another.

Dearest Reader,

Welcome. The pages of this tome, whether fresh from print or aged and fragile from use, will take you to the fair town of Ipswich. I had the pleasure of spending some time there myself and discovered a few interesting things. The inhabitants were a proud people, most certainly set in their ways, no matter how flawed. There was much unhappiness, but deep down inside each and every member of the community, there was a desire to be better. Do we not all have that desire? Yet worry and caution and fear and embarrassment all prevent it from realizing its true potential. Throw those to the wind, grab my hand, and step with me into the sunlight, dear friend. The world truly looks beautiful from up here.

Yours Most Sincerely,
Perran Nemerov

Now, until the break of day,
Through this house each fairy stray.
To the best bride-bed will we,
Which by us shall blessed be;
And the issue there create
Ever shall be fortunate.
So shall all the couples three
Ever true in loving be;
And the blots of Nature's hand
Shall not in their issue stand;
Never mole, hare lip, nor scar,
Nor mark prodigious, such as are
Despised in nativity,
Shall upon their children be.
With this field-dew consecrate,
Every fairy take his gait;
And each several chamber bless,
Through this palace, with sweet peace;
And the owner of it blest
Ever shall in safety rest.
Trip away;
Make no stay;
Meet me all by break of day.

V.ii.31-53 *A Midsummer's Night Dream* by William Shakespeare.

PROLOGUE

There were no eyes as startlingly blue as Perran Nemerov's. Even in the cold mist of the December morning as he strode up the graveyard hill under a weeping grey sky, his eyes were a sight to behold. Under the single, lonely, lifeless tree at the crest of the hill, kneeling before a newly prepared gravestone, was a beautiful young red headed girl, no older than eight. He approached slowly through the mist so as not to startle the mourning child. She wore a dress, likely her Sunday finest, and held her head low as her wavy red locks fell over her shoulders, dangling as low as her spirits.

She looked up when Perran was still several paces away. He held his hands together in front of him and bowed his head of wavy dark brown hair in respect. Appearing to be no more than twenty, he still seemed old to the innocent young girl – an unknown stranger. He wore no shoes, only a plain white tunic and brown pants that were several inches too short. Despite all this, his outfit did not seem out of place; his eyes seemed to make everything okay.

The girl said nothing, tears still streaming down from swollen red eyes.

"Hello, little girl," he said. "Who are you visiting today?" There was concern riding his words.

The girl turned to the headstone in front of which she knelt. There engraved on the stone were the two names of the parents who had left their single young daughter behind. Perran nodded in solemn understanding. He knew too well the pain of loss and had lost many that he cared about throughout his years — more than he ever wanted to count.

"I'm Perran." He stuck out his hand, and she halfheartedly extended her own. When she pulled her hand back, there was a single small sunflower in her palm. She looked at him, confused. He had not been holding anything. Perran shrugged. "I know it hurts. It's supposed to hurt... it means that your love for them is true." The girl gently placed the flower at the base of the gravestone, turning her head to make sure it was positioned just so, her tears dripping quietly onto the Earth.

The quiet young girl maintained her silence as Perran sat down crossed legged on the ground next to her. "And as much as it hurts, it will ease. You'll see that they live on in other ways," he sighed. "But until then, just know you are never alone."

The young girl looked over at her strange companion and tried meekly to smile. "I hope not," she said.

Naturally, people talked. They wondered why a strange young man was spending so much time with the young orphan. They were seen all about town, always together. Since she had met him, she learned that he was new to town but did not have family or friends of his own, much like herself. He helped her through her time of mourning and was with her when she needed a shoulder to cry on. Granted, it was an odd sight to behold — the strange blue-eyed boy almost in adulthood walking down the street with the girl half his size, not yet learning the realities of adolescence. Still, although people talked, no one got involved. People avoided orphans and tragedy like they avoided an infected dog or unbathed beggar. Most considered them one in the same.

Perran taught her to ride a bicycle and swim in the creek and smiled and joked with her until she was finally able to laugh out loud once again. They became fast friends, and while the little girl moved in with her aunt and uncle, Perran became a parental figure and companion for her. They talked about the issues of the world, debated their favorite colors with more detailed reasoning than required, and always argued about what a certain cloud should be named.

Years later, in the lazy sunset of a perfect summer day, the two friends decided to go for a walk through the park, one of their favorite pastimes. The little girl had grown since their first encounter and was approaching Perran in height, which he noticed when they both sat down in the grass, leaning back to name the clouds. The sky that night was a sight to behold. The clouds were painted orange and violet by the evening sky, like frosting spread with a giant knife in colorful swirls or watercolors splashed upon a fading blue canvas.

The girl turned, supporting her head with her propped arm, and looked at Perran, who was unusually quiet that day.

"Is something wrong?" She turned her head to the side, curious. She had never seen him act differently before. He did not look at her but continued to stare upward, his blue eyes matching the expanse above.

"I have to go now," he said simply.

"Go where? Can I come?" she didn't understand what he was saying.

"I'm afraid not, my friend, I have to go to a place far from here. There is someone who needs my help."

The girl was disbelieving. Perran was her constant, her foundation. He had been the support she needed at a dark time. She still wasn't entirely sure where he had come from, but strangely, she never cared enough to inquire. She looked her mysterious companion in the eyes. He finally turned and met her gaze.

"But..." She could feel the threat of tears building up as a lump in throat. "Why?"

Perran knew she wouldn't understand at first, and it pained him to see her upset. Instead of answering her question, which really had no suitable answer, he said, "I have a gift for you." He reached around to his pocket while the sun ducked behind a cloud on its descent toward the horizon.

"You know you don't have to." She was holding back tears. They had friendship beyond formalities such as gift giving.

"I know, but I want you to have something for when I am gone." He pulled out a book from his back pocket. It was small and had a leather bound cover with ornate gold lettering stamped into the front. "Here."

The girl took the book in her hands and read the title, Shakespeare's Sonnets. She opened the page and gently leafed through, noticing that Perran had drawn decorations around each of the poems. Floral patterns with a subtle tribal influence surrounded the titles and concepts of love and tragedy that Shakespeare spoke of, vines winding around the sides of the page and giving the book an almost organic feel. She looked at her friend, struggling madly to hold back the sobs.

"Thank you," she managed to say, clenching her jaw to keep her emotions from pouring out like a river breaking through its dam.

"I have to go now," said he. The little girl who was no longer so little began to tear up.

"I know." With all her might, she held back from weeping, "I don't want to say goodbye."

"Then don't, my friend," Perran said, standing, "Perhaps in another life, our paths will cross again."

He kissed her on the forehead and started to walk away as the sun came out from behind one of the clouds. The field lit up, waving yellow and gold like an ocean gilded in the warm midsummer breeze. She smiled back, tears finally emerging, as Perran walked through the field, into the woods, and out of sight.

"Perhaps."

PART ONE

Mary

Few sounds cause as much inner anguish in teenagers as that of a screeching alarm clock on a weekday morning. It is that sound that Mary Augustine woke to on her eighteenth birthday, and as expected, she rushed to end the audible torture as soon as possible with a swift whack of her hand.

She rose from her bed and heard a crunch underfoot. The printed pages of a internet fan fiction novel she had been reading the night before had fallen to the floor, so she bent and carefully moved the pile to her already messy desk. She spent every night eagerly reading the latest Harry Potter fan fiction printed off hastily in Courier New (so it would look like it was fresh from the typewriter). She paused, looking at the pile, but decided to rearrange the papers later; it was her eighteenth birthday, and she could allow herself some relaxation.

"Mary! Wake up!" Her mother knew that Mary woke to her alarm clock without fail. Yet for some reason, she felt the need to shriek up to her daughter from the kitchen below. Perhaps it was her way of saying "Good morning, dear, I love you so," but Mary would never know. She liked to think as much though.

After a shower much too quick to go beyond cold water, she walked down the stairs and into the kitchen. Most teenagers her age would find balloons and a pile of presents as their parents tried to desperately cling to a childhood long past. Mary, on the other hand, found a single rectangular gift wrapped in newspaper sitting on the aging linoleum island that acted as a breakfast bar. She delicately unwrapped it, careful not to rip any of the paper as she slowly pried the tape off. When she was done, she held a small plastic makeup kit, likely from the dollar store. Mary never wore makeup and couldn't decide whether the gift was her mother's indifference or a hint. She put it out of her mind.

"Thanks, Mom."

Laura Augustine bit into her slightly soggy buttered toast and looked over her newspaper to smile at her daughter, "Anytime, kiddo."

"Can I skip school today? It is a big birthday year after all," Mary asked.

"Ha." Laura went back to her newspaper, chuckling at her daughter's absurd request. Mary didn't care much for school. She was only interested in her stories – fantasies that took her far from this world where she was an awkward, lanky teenager with nary a friend. Her sandy blond hair and green eyes were fair enough, but her lack of confidence and questionable choice of clothes left her in the background of the vibrant scenery that was a teenager's discovery of themselves, their bodies, and their own personal "look." Mary was more interested in discovering who stole the Crown of Fire in the Third World series than the latest neon fashions at Urban Outfitters.

Pushing the makeup kit out of her way, Mary took out a bowl to eat her usual breakfast of grits and brown sugar. Her mother gave her grief for being a New Englander who liked grits, but Mary found the texture much more interesting than mushy oatmeal. As she ate spoonfuls of her concoction, she let the dread of the day's coming Spanish test wash over her. College was not part of her life plan at the moment, so grades shouldn't have bothered her as much as they did, but it was painful to fail at something as simple as language when her life revolved around literature and storytelling. She had yet to discuss her plans with her mother, who Mary was certain would not be pleased that her daughter wanted to bypass college and become a fantasy novelist. Eventually, she would reveal her plans, but it would be a disastrous conversation that was very easily put off time and time again.

Mary ate her breakfast in silence, no questions from her mother about her birthday plans or what was coming that day in school. Laura already knew that her daughter didn't have many friends, and it was that knowledge and a sense of indifference that kept her silent as she perused the headlines of the day in the local paper, brushing her dark hair out of her eyes between every few sips of coffee. Laura was only forty-two, young to have an eighteen-year-old. She had mid-length dark brown hair and piercing green eyes. She kept very fit and wore clothes that made people aware of her trim figure without showing off or being obscene. She would have been beautiful if she only smiled, but she chose to go about her day with a constant indifference. During the daytime hours, she substituted at the local private school, and afterward, her job was to drink cheap flavored vodka and watch trashy television. Every morning, she would have her coffee and scrutinize the local paper. Apparently, winter caused icy roads. What a groundbreaking report, she thought sarcastically.

"Okay, Mom, if you aren't going to waiver in your convictions, I suppose I have no choice but to attend to my classes now," Mary said in a mock British accent as she put away her dishes and began to gather her schoolbooks into her backpack.

God, is she awkward, Laura thought, but she instead said, "Okay, dear. Have a good birthday. I'll see you tonight."

Mary zipped her puffy winter coat and threw her backpack over her shoulders, ready to brave the crisp January air. Just the day before it had been mild enough to walk to school without a coat at all, but that's New England for you. She opened the door and was immediately greeted by the bitter wind. She slowly made her way toward Ipswich High School, the public school where she was finishing the second half of her senior year.

Ipswich was a traditional New England town – a forest of trees and winding streets, colonial era homes retrofitted with modern amenities, aged infrastructure, and the occasional early eighties development that never took off as planned. It was divided down the middle by High Street, which ran parallel to the Merrimack River. On the northern side of High Street, which shared a coastline of the river, was the downtown area, as well as the expensively renovated houses, former homes of captains and revolutionary generals. This is where those who attended the local private school, Saint Andrews Academy, lived. On the south side were the suburban developments, and while there were some surviving colonial homes among the aging developments, it was primarily mass produced homes, reminiscent of the days when an entire house could be bought from a Sears catalog. The south side housed the public school and the majority of its students.

The divide was known and used as a status monitor in the town. To move from the south side to the north was an admirable feat, a sign of success, but you would sooner move to Canada than relocate from a northside mansion to a southside bungalow. Running down the middle, perpendicular to High Street and the Merrimack, was State Street, and the businesses and public areas around it were common to all residents of Ipswich, northsiders and southsiders alike. Included was Angela's Diner, across from the gas station at the intersection of the two main roads, as well as the downtown shops, all housed in traditional brick buildings looming over brick sidewalks and cobblestone streets. A photograph of downtown Ipswich could easily be mistaken for a European village.

Down South State Street was hidden a dirt turnoff, which led to the expansive Maudson State Park. Once home to an extremely wealthy family, the 300-acre plot of land that incorporated fields, forests, and overgrown rose gardens was a popular spot among the townspeople, though little known to tourists. The park was so large that even though everyone visited on a regular basis, one would be hard pressed to run into a neighbor while walking the endless mulched trails. It was a popular spot for experimental students to try drugs and alcohol for the first time, though their presence did detract from the park's beauty since they mostly kept to themselves.

Such was Ipswich, a town of beauty and community; effortlessly merging history, nature, and commerce in a picturesque package. A deeper look would reveal micro communities, endlessly battling rumors, and differences of opinion, bitter and unhappy bubbling just beneath the surface. But then again, who can say that is different from any other town in the world?

When Mary finally arrived at school, she found that as usual, she was fifteen minutes late to class. Spanish was her first class of the day, and she was barely passing it. With little regard for her academic future, this should not have bothered her, yet the looming test that she was completely unprepared for made her hands clammy and her heart quicken. She walked briskly on the over vacuumed dark blue carpet worn to thread by the endless footsteps it endured every day, past the 1970s vomit green lockers that adorned the walls, and into the brightly lit Spanish classroom that was decorated with colorful posters of children from Spanish speaking countries. It reminded her of a preschool classroom, except instead of play-dough, there was a very real, very difficult test waiting for her on her desk.

Later, she should would realize the importance of education, among many other life-altering revelations. This would come long after the Spanish test that she was about to bomb, her shift at Movie Express that night, a boring dinner of sauerkraut and hot dogs, and night after night of the latest in internet fan fiction. It was a ways off, sure, but the process was about to begin nevertheless. Its catalyst arrived at the Ipswich town line the moment Mary put her pencil to her paper – a catalyst that would slip unnoticed through the town, forever changing its inhabitants. Like everyone else in Ipswich, Mary was still blissfully unaware – but not for long.

Laura

Moments after her daughter closed the back door and was on her way to school, the freezing January air wafted over Laura where she sat. It mocked her, as if to say *You can't stay inside forever, you have to meet me out here sooner or later.* And with that, Laura rose and proceeded to finish preparing for her day. She was scheduled to substitute at nine o'clock at Saint Andrews on the northside and was already running a few minutes behind schedule.

Quickly applying the little makeup that she wore on a daily basis, Laura's mind drifted to her ex-husband, Joseph. He had left almost ten years ago, quite suddenly and quite completely. So completely that she had not heard from him in almost all of those ten years. He wrote letters to Mary for the first couple of months but stopped without explanation in the middle of their correspondence. Through mutual acquaintances,

Laura learned to suspect that Joseph was somewhere in Los Angeles chasing down wannabe actresses. She was still in love with him and would probably take him back if he returned, though she would never admit that to herself. It was not that she wasn't hurt, but she missed the past and never accepted the finality of its loss.

Shaking the thoughts of Joseph from her mind, Laura grabbed her coat, scarf, hat, and mittens. She looked as if she was prepared to walk all the way to the northside, when in fact she was just walking out to the car, a 1999 Subaru. Cold affected her more than most, and she always overdressed for it. In the spring time, Laura would still be bundled up, even as the mercury was reaching for the sixties.

The drive to Saint Andrews was one of the prettiest in town. High Street was lined with perfectly restored colonial homes. Laura loved the crisp white Greek revivals with dark shutters topped with pitch black roofs peaking at heights reaching for the clouds. The barn red deeded half houses loomed overhead, featuring manicured lawns, clean even in the winter as the blades yellowed and waited for the eminent arrival of spring. She turned off High Street and into the northside of town, out of the dense downtown area and toward the timeless Saint Andrews campus.

Saint Andrews sat on rolling hills in the Ipswich Woods. It was comprised of a dozen different buildings, mostly brick, all mansion sized. These were connected by a series of cobblestone walkways and bridges to span the creek that wound through the grounds. In the center of the campus was a Great Hall, the largest of the buildings, and it housed the cafeteria, main offices, and music classrooms. It was here that

Laura had to check in in order to get her room assignment for the day. Usually this was decided based on which underpaid instructor had a little too much single malt scotch the night before and called out with the "flu."

She walked past the soaring windows in the hallway and into the waiting room just outside the main offices. The reception desk was just outside the locked door to the inner offices. A stout woman sat behind the desk, typing away at a new Apple computer. She wore a dark red power suit (red and white were the colors of Saint Andrews) and glasses with sequins (or were they diamonds?) encrusted on the sides.

"Good morning, Kathy," Laura said, already bored with the job without having even received her assignment yet.

"What a pleasure it is to see you again, Ms. Augustine." Kathy was formal not out of spite but out of habit. "My gracious, you must be freezing! Well no bother, you're taking over for Khandoker today, and his room is very well heated."

Laura grabbed the master key that allowed all personnel into the faculty lounge (or faculty parlor as it was called among the permanent members of the staff) and bathrooms around campus. Erkut Khandoker taught calculus, something Laura didn't even have a chance at grasping. Normally if the subject were something she still retained knowledge of, Laura would do her best to keep the class occupied and get a discussion going that she could moderate. With something complicated like calculus, however, she was forced to make the students quietly complete the assigned work or else let them work on other homework amongst themselves. The latter option generally led to a very loud free-for-all that she could not imagine was very productive. Still, she generally said nothing.

She got paid regardless of the productivity of her pupils.

A private high school was a funny place. Freshly buffed tiles clicked in response to every footstep, and there were immaculate brick walls and soaring peaked windows and cathedral ceilings. Such a beautiful setting was the habitat of the most despicable creature: the high school student. Lacking any sense of self, they leeched off the insecurities of others. Ever criticizing, they latched on to the smallest of errors of their peers and exploited them into campus wide gossip. Laura always beamed with happiness when she discovered a gem among the crowd, one that wouldn't stoop to her low expectations and stereotypes of the age group.

Thankfully, her classroom for the day was in the closest building to the Great Hall, a ten-room red brick behemoth with twenty-foot ceilings and larger than life front doors. Once inside, Laura put her things down at the missing instructor's desk. Substituting was an odd experience. Here she was, given complete access to this person's – this stranger's – world. Most instructors, she found, kept personal belongings at work, everything from iPods to love letters to contraception (which she hoped dearly was to be used on their colleagues and not their students; but being a substitute, it wasn't her concern). She never snooped or took anything. These are just the things she inadvertently came across while looking for a pencil or extra box of staples. God knows what she could find if she went snooping. Compromising photographs? Heirloom diamonds? Missing paintings from the Isabella Stuart Gardner heist?

Almost as soon as she got settled, the electronic PA system chimed, for long gone were the screeching of school bells.

Within moments, the classroom was filling with students around the same age as her daughter. The boys wore slacks and boat shoes; the girls wore skirts and black flats. Their top halves open to free choice, as long as it incorporated some form of red and white, usually a white polo with red logo or school patch sewn on. Laura noticed that one boy, a handsome shaggy haired fellow with the most piercing blue eyes, had moccasins instead of boat shoes, and his white tunic shirt was untucked and adorned with a very ragged blood red scarf that was likely too informal for the administration's preferences. She shrugged it off, however, as it didn't bother her and would likely just cause an argument and headache if she were to say anything about it.

"Everyone quiet down!" Laura projected firmly, but she never yelled, for it was too much effort. "I have seen most of you before, but in case any of you don't know me, I'm Ms. Augustine. Your instructor, Dr. Khandoker, is out sick today, and unfortunately I haven't found any lesson plans yet. Can someone tell me if there are any ongoing projects or assignments you can work on during class today?"

She could almost hear the janitor scratching his chin two rooms down the hallway, the class got so quiet. These kids are about to go out into the real world, Laura thought to herself. Why in God's name are they so shy?

"Anyone? Prior?" Laura looked at Tanner Prior. She knew him as one of the popular soccer players in the school's most desirable clique, but from classes she had with him in the past, she knew he wasn't a complete idiot like most of his teammates. Hopefully, he would be honest about the assignments the class had, as it was clear that they were hiding something.

"Uh... I don't think so." What a terrible liar, Laura noted.

"Okay, Barber, what's the assignment?" Laura turned and looked at Timothy Barber. He, too, played soccer, but he was also one of the theatre junkies, an odd crossover that could only happen at a school like Saint Andrews where participation in sports was mandatory. He was of moderate height with classic soccer build and cropped dark hair, contrasting his kind, green eyes that were flanked by eyelashes dark enough to sometimes give the illusion of eye shadow in the right light. The theatre kids generally didn't mind academics, so she was hoping she would have better luck with him.

"Er... well... I mean, we have this one in-book problem set, but it's not due for a long time. I don't think he would have us work on it today." Barber obviously felt compelled to be honest but had to stifle it so his classmates wouldn't skewer him after class.

"Ah, it's settled then. Everyone take out the problem set Mr. Barber speaks of and work on that quietly until the end of class. I don't want to have to send anyone to the office." It was an empty threat, for Laura would never send anyone to the office. Just as she went to get out her latest Nora Roberts book and settle into Mr. Khandoker's high backed chair with swivel and lumbar support, she noticed that the shaggy haired boy had his hand raised. He didn't have any books or supplies, and while everyone else around him was starting to work on their calculus, typing numbers into calculators, and regurgitating the numbers onto paper, the boy with the blue eyes just waited patiently to be called on. Laura acknowledged him with a nod.

"Madam Augustine," he began. The boy seemed oddly familiar.

"Ms. Augustine is fine, thank you."

"My apologies. Ms. Augustine, today is my first day. I don't have a book, nor do I know which problems Mr. Barber mentioned," he said, pronouncing every syllable carefully, speaking with grace yet seeming completely natural and at ease at the same time.

"I would give you the assignment, but I'm afraid I don't know it. Let's see... why don't you share materials with Mr. Barber for today, then, and hopefully when Mr. Khandoker returns tomorrow, he can fill you in completely."

The boy nodded, a slight smile on his face. He quickly and quietly picked up his chair and brought it over to Timothy's desk, and the two of them worked together on the calculus throughout the class. When Laura looked up from her book, she noticed the new kid appeared to be quite smart, as he would constantly point out mistakes in his partner's work. He seemed to do so kindly enough, though, as Timothy seemed to be getting along fine with him. Any other soccer player who was corrected by a new student, let alone a slightly androgynous one, would not have taken so kindly.

As soon as it had started, the class was over, and the electronic chime alerted the students to move to their next class. As they were exiting, Laura asked one of the girls when Khandoker's next class was. The girl informed her that he only taught the one AP calculus class, which meant that Laura got to leave early today and get home before lunchtime. Leaving early because an instructor doesn't have a full load was one of her favorite surprises.

Gathering her things together, she was already dreading the frigid walk back to her station wagon. She carefully wrapped her scarf around her neck and wondered what she would do with the extra time she had in the day. Were her earnings greater than that of a substitute teacher, she would treat herself to a spa or a movie. Things being as they were, she decided to drive home and pop in an over-watched DVD and have an afternoon drink. It was Tuesday, but it would be noon by the time she arrived home, or so she justified. It was an innocent habit, honest. She just needed to escape now and then – more often now than then.

The warmth of her house thawed her extremities as soon as she stepped inside, and soon the lemon flavored vodka and Diet Coke was joining her for a lazy afternoon. The tang of the citrus mingled with the burn of the cheap vodka snapping at her throat on its way down, though eventually a warmth grew from her stomach that drowned out the taste. The Three Amigos with Steve Martin was on queue for today, and thirty minutes into the movie, she was asleep in the old armchair facing the TV. Immediately, or so it seemed (for the truth is, she was asleep until even the TV got tired of repeating the music for the title menu of the DVD), her daughter Mary burst in the front door. Laura stirred, not wasted but still tipsy from her afternoon beverages.

"Home already, Mom?"

"Y-yeah. Have been for a while. Must have fallensleep watching TV." Laura rubbed her eyes, weary with the grogginess that so often accompanies naps.

"It's nice you had a short day."

Laura become more alert. Everything rushed back. It was Mary's birthday. It was a weekday, not a Friday night.

"How was your birthday at school? How did that Spanish test go?" Laura walked to the cabinet and got herself a glass of water. "Want anything?"

"I'm fine, thanks." Mary looked nervous. "My day was okay, I guess. I uh... I didn't do so great on the test."

"How not great?"

"I failed it." She looked humiliated. Laura didn't want to scold her on her birthday, but Spanish was the class that was keeping her grade point average down. She knew her daughter was capable of better.

"Mary..." Laura was halfhearted and didn't know quite what to say. She just wanted another drink, but that would have to wait until Mary went up to her room.

"Whatever. It doesn't matter anyway," Mary said, sulking up the stairs and into the confines of her room where she would spend the rest of her birthday not with friends or enjoying the freedom of turning eighteen and becoming an adult, not buying scratch tickets or dirty magazines or cigarettes or registering to vote. Instead, Laura's daughter sat at her desk, rearranged the crumpled pages of Larry Hatter and Magical Triangle Lifeforce, a story written by a fifteen-year-old on his parents' computer, and read until the sun set. She sat alone at the desk while Laura below let the warm waves of vodka splash repeatedly over her consciousness, numbing existence into nothing but a soft hum.

Tanner

"Shut the hell up, faggot!"

"Why don't you make me?"

"Because your mom promised me a BJ if I was nice to you."

"Oh you're going to fu—"

Tanner Prior watched one of his teammates tackle the other. They punched and kicked at each other, scuffled on the ground, and eventually gave up and started laughing. Such is life, Tanner thought, a mantra he often repeated in his head to help him shrug the weight of the world off his shoulders. All varsity sports were the same; there was a fraternal atmosphere about it all. Tanner liked feeling like he had a bunch of brothers he could always count on, though he wasn't as completely dedicated to it as some of the other guys. He still had a life outside of soccer and preferred to keep it to himself.

Tanner was one of the better soccer players on the team. At just under six feet tall, he had the classic runner's build. He was thin enough for great speed and be light on his feet, but defined and strong enough to take a hit when needed. He had short, messy, dirty blond hair and big green eyes that drew the girls in like mosquitoes on a summer night. Much to their dismay, they were almost completely ignored, which of course made them chase him more. They, like most others, didn't know much about Tanner, which only added to his mysterious allure.

His love of art was one thing almost no one knew about. The other teammates would latch on to that and give him hell for the rest of his life if they found out he painted. Such is life. Oftentimes, instead of doing his homework after practice, he would put on a Velvet Underground record in his attic bedroom and get out the canvas and acrylic paints he bought while he was in Boston one weekend the year before.

He tried everything – landscapes, self portraits, abstractions. He just had an intensely burning creative fire within that he had to release to keep from going crazy, and he couldn't do that on the soccer field. Painting made him feel like he was working on his internal battles. Every teenager goes through the struggle of finding themselves, and Tanner wanted to figure it out with canvas and brushes and paint. Unfortunately, he had yet to come to any conclusions and sometimes wondered if he wasn't just confusing himself more. He considered the possibility that he already knew what he was, the sports star his father wanted. It didn't feel right, though, and the walk-in closet filled to the brim with paintings in all different stages of completion was a testament to that.

His father, Gavin Prior, was a very stern man. Having lost his brother and wife in an alcohol related car accident years ago, he had become a recluse. His brother was a star athlete and went to college on sports scholarships. Tanner reminded Gavin of his brother in an uncanny way. As such, he insisted that sports be Tanner's top priority, expecting his brother to somehow live vicariously through his son. Over schoolwork, friends, and other commitments, sports came first. Tanner only saw his father as suffocating.

"Hey, who's the girly boy?" Rich Gervez called out to his teammates, nodding with his head across the field to the boy walking with a book toward the woods. He had a shaggy head of dark hair and was wearing clothes that weren't all together out of place, just somehow... different.

"Anyone know who the new kid is?" Tanner looked back at his team.

"He looks like a Brit," Kieran O'Connell, the Irish exchange student, student called out. None of his American teammates understood.

"He looks like my sister."

Almost as if he heard, the new boy turned down the path that passed right by the soccer field. As he got closer, the boys saw that although he was slightly androgynous, he had a very strong jaw, almost white blue eyes, and a graceful masculinity that would undoubtedly have any of their girlfriends swooning at the sight of him. A painfully cold January breeze swept across the field, quickly eliminating the comfort of what had been a mild day.

As he was about to turn down a path that took him back into campus, he looked directly at the boy who had likened him to his sister, and barely above a whisper but loud enough for everyone to hear, he said, "You, sir, are unfit for any place but hell."

Normally, the boys would have laughed, but for some reason, the newcomer's intensity and absolute confidence made his retort even more chilling than the sudden change in temperature.

"C'mon, guys, let's go!" Timothy Barber called out, already walking away.

Math and science did not agree with Tanner. He found English interesting but never put in the effort to discover much about it. His time was spent at practice – well, practice and painting. It didn't help that the strangely creepy English teacher, Ms. Ramsay, was having them read old plays written before he was born.

"Pupils, kindly present your tomes from last semester. Today I will be distributing the tragic tale of Oedipus Rex, the first in our semester of Drama, which will continue with Oscar Wilde and conclude with the bard, Shakespeare himself." She walked so gracefully across the classroom it almost looked like she was gliding. The soccer team was convinced that she was certifiably insane. Her eccentric draped clothing and frizzy red hair did little to sway their opinion.

Normal grammar was difficult enough for Tanner, let alone translated works and Olde English. His buddy Timothy ate it up, though. In the off-season Timothy was a part of the school drama club and was always more of a theater kid. The school's mandatory sports program ensured he would play for the soccer team, for which he had a natural talent. Tanner was glad that sports were required. He and Timothy were always close friends, the type that you could tell your secrets to without fear of ridicule. Timothy was the only one who knew about his paintings, and naturally, he supported his friend.

School that day was a series of blurs, just one mechanized chime indicating the end of class and start of another. He didn't understand any of it, and he was thankful for the substitute in Calculus that spared him the torture of meaningless numbers and symbols. During what turned into a free period for him, however, the new kid from earlier in the day buddied up with Timothy since he didn't yet have materials for the class. This pissed Tanner off to no end, though he could not articulate why.

After class, he approached Timothy. He swung his backpack over his dress code compliant shoulder and chided him.

"So, making friends with the new kid, I see." His tone was accusatory.

"Hey, Tan, don't get like that. He's actually not bad. He seems really smart. Said his family travels a lot."

"Yeah, well, something doesn't seem right about him. Did you hear what he said to Sam out in the field? That was weird, man." He pulled out his cellphone and checked for text messages – nothing important.

"I don't know. I think we should just give him a chance. Maybe he could be cool, you know? Put yourself in his shoes." Timothy pulled his phone out as well. Tanner didn't notice the constant imitation.

"We'll see." The two walked over to the field where they would play their last exhibition game of the year. The season had ended a month before, with them losing the title by one game. Next year's team would likely start practice before school was even out. Their coach was crazy, anyway, with unreasonable intensity. As it was, they were still playing exhibition games with only the most die hard of other schools simply so they could end their season on a win. Layered in skin-tight athletic clothes designed to keep in warmth, they looked like soldiers in training as they acted on the whims of their hyper masculine coach.

After they won the exhibition (much to the pleasure of Coach Reinbeck), Tanner walked home to his house in downtown Ipswich. It was a single-family Federal style, painted a pale yellow with trim as white as the clouds. On a clear day, the silky blue sky was a perfect compliment to colorful house, which stood tall over the brick sidewalk. It was one street away from all the downtown shops and galleries and a short walk to the boardwalk that wound along the bank of the Merrimack River. The boardwalk was generally very quiet at night, and whenever he felt the need to escape, Tanner would walk along its edge, noting the colors that the sunset played upon the river's surface. He was lucky when his free time, the daylight, and good weather coincided to afford him such pleasurable outdoor strolls, for like the alignment of the planets, this was very rare. As it were, it was already dark out thanks to the early nights of New England winters, and his father was waiting for him in the parlor right inside their large front door.

"Well?" Gavin Prior asked, muting the television as his son walked in and turning to him with an expectant look upon his face.

"Yeah, we won." He was already bored with it. "We knew we would, though. Governor's Institute has had a weak season."

"Always so modest, Tanner. You'll market well." Gavin was already thinking of his son's future as a professional athlete. "What was the score?"

"Six-four. We were down in the beginning of the second half, but Coach put Timothy in instead of Riley, which helped us turn it around. He's so aggressive as a forward. They weren't expecting it from him." His father didn't reply but nodded, imagining the game and undoubtedly fantasizing about his brother playing alongside his son's teammates. "Well, Dad, I have to go do my homework. Big day tomorrow."

Tanner walked through the parlor and into the kitchen, which had been renovated the year before and now featured polished marble countertops, a six-burner stove, and other modern amenities hidden behind the façade of dark cherry wood cabinetry. He grabbed a soda from the fridge, as well as the remains of a falafel sandwich he had bought the day before, and walked the two flights of stairs up to his bedroom, which had previously been the attic before the house was remodeled.

It had retained much of its charm. When the renovations were being completed, Gavin had allowed Tanner to make all the decisions regarding his private space. He had opted to keep the original ceiling beams exposed and the floors untreated, minus a fresh coat of paint to prevent splinters or other maladies. The original and classic feel the room therefore maintained was a welcome catalyst for Tanner's creative process. His surroundings reminded him of simpler days, which brought forth inspiration for many of his paintings.

He put his dinner on his desk, an antique writing piece that came with the house and was too large to take down the narrow staircases, and got his painting supplies out. Suddenly, he was filled with inexplicable frustration and had to get all on the canvas. After an hour or two, he had made significant progress, but the dim light overhead began to flicker. Knowing that he only had a few minutes before it blew completely and left him in darkness, Tanner washed his hands in the cast-iron sink in the attached bathroom.

The moment he walked out, there was a flash and a pop, and the the room went black. After a moment, his eyes adjusted, and the yellow glow of the streetlights below filtered in through his thin curtains. Instead of finding a replacement bulb, he simply stripped down and got in bed, drifting to the numbness of sleep as his half finished painting started to dry.

George

It appeared that the remains of someone's home fries had experienced a mini breakfast-plate blizzard, each chunk of grilled potato and grease covered in sugar that looked like snow drifts. George Rutherford, who worked at Angela's Diner, cleared the plate off the table and rolled his eyes. Most likely the culprit was a too-skinny private school princess who was tempted by the food but wanted to "kill it" with the sugar to make it undesirable. That way, she wouldn't give in to temptation and lose her rail-like figure. He had seen it a hundred times.

The best part about working at Angela's (besides the free meals) was having a birds eye view of the Ipswich social strata. Saint Andrews and Ipswich High students alike enjoyed breakfast before school, the local workers from the southside came in for lunch, and ritzy northsiders often brought their families for dinner, especially if they had small children that wouldn't be presentable in the fancy restaurants they frequented with their equally ritzy business associates. It was one of the few places beyond the limits of downtown Ipswich where the community convened. A stranger looking into the diner might fall under the vastly miscalculated opinion that Ipswich was extremely tight-knit and blissfully happy. Such an image gave George hope, which he otherwise had little of.

George had graduated from Ipswich High School nearly ten years prior and almost immediately upon graduation had decided to forgo college and move to New York City to make it as a film maker. He struggled for the first few months but was extremely dedicated. Taking unpaid internships, fetching coffee, and shining shoes just to make the proper contacts that drove the industry, he was a young man with a dream. Fortune eventually visited George one day when a young man learned of his aspirations and set up an appointment for him with the Vice President of Production at MTV networks. It was George's dream opportunity – the type of opportunity that happens only in movies, a chance meeting leading to the job of his dreams. His hard work and sacrifices were all about to pay off, and he was ready to celebrate.

That night, George and his roommates hit the town hard and went out to various hip midtown nightclubs to celebrate his impending success. They had drinks, drugs, and girls galore, happy to be in a city of sin in the prime of their lives. George could recall little of the night, but if he had he would remember the tequila shots on the roof of a forty-story building as the sun rose over Queens three hours before his scheduled appointment at MTV.

He awoke the next day at one in the afternoon in a stranger's apartment. His head felt like it was about to split open, and despite being severely dehydrated and hungry, the thought of putting any food or drink in his mouth made him sick to his stomach. It was only an hour later as he was cleaning himself up in his too-small bathroom back at his apartment that he remembered the appointment. The disappointment washed over him in waves and never truly receded completely. He had, of course, called and tried to reschedule, but businessmen in New York were unforgiving, especially the ones in the entertainment business. He kept at it for a few more months in the city, making halfhearted attempts to land jobs on cable television shows and local news, but even his lowered standards yielded no success.

Eventually, George could no longer stand the disappointment. Dejected, he gave up and hopped on the Chinatown bus back to Boston, where his parents were waiting to bring him back home to Ipswich, where he had been ever since working at Angela's Diner by day and delivering pizzas at night. George had to work both jobs just to make enough money to pay for his basement apartment in a multi-family house on the southside. He couldn't have borne the embarrassment of living with his parents on top of having to face his failure in New York.

As George continued to clean the table of the recent party, he noticed that the young future anorexic had not made too much of a mess on her table, and he was able to wipe it down and replace the flatware quickly enough that the next patrons did not have to wait to sit down. Four private school boys (athletes, it seemed) sat down and began looking through the limited breakfast menu.

"Tan, you have something on your face," the one with the buzzcut said to his friend.

"Oh, yeah. I had to uh... repaint part of my room last night."

"Yeah? I don't remember your room being bright orange."

"What the fuck do you know?"

George decided to give them a minute to finish their inevitable argument. The private school boys were all so brimming with unjustified entitlement and pride. They always ended up challenging each other to a yelling match, but as soon as a southsider walked in, they would remember their common superiority and revert to being buddies in no time. Just as they were starting to escalate their volume, Mary Augustine, the awkward girl from the movie rental store, walked in alone. They turned to look at her and rolled their eyes in response. Suddenly, their argument was over, and they began discussing their final soccer game held the night before.

George sometimes chatted with Mary at her job, but she always seemed like the type of person who started crawling in her skin during conversations with another person. Still, he knew that he was probably one of the only people she felt comfortable enough to have an actual conversation with. He also couldn't deny that although she was awkward, she did have genuinely unique insights into the films and literature that he was interested in.

Barry Ann Girard took care of Mary, sweeping her away to an empty table near the window. She was the girl's Spanish instructor and usually worked nights, but it was the beginning of a three-day weekend, and she had picked up the extra morning shifts to help pay for her upcoming wedding.

George liked the people he worked with, for the most part. Those who were taking the job for extra money like Barry Ann were generally intelligent beyond the needs of the job and could provide good conversation when a lull in business allowed it. There were a couple of employees, however, whose highest aspiration was to serve fried foods at the town diner. He had a hard time relating to them, and every misstep or mistake they made hit him the wrong way, as he had no one to empathize. He still didn't associate himself with them, even as he slowly joined their ranks, lacking any further aspirations or ambitions of his own. George had been shot down too many times.

After he had helped seat a few more patrons and cleared the remaining tables, George decided to go over and talk to Mary. She looked so lonely eating her usual order of grits and brown sugar alone at the window, and he had just seen a new movie he was dying to discuss with someone.

"Hey there," he said, trying too hard to be casual, so as not to scare her back into her shell.

"Oh, hello, George." She looked back at him, expecting him to ask if the food was okay or if she needed ketchup.

"Mind if I sit?" Completely taken aback, Mary opened her eyes wide as she tried to comprehend the rules of the social situation. She wasn't as bad as she thought at socializing. She just didn't have the confidence and was convinced she would make a fool of herself.

"S-sure, by all means." A little too eager perhaps, but she was new at this.

"Hey, you didn't happen to see Abandoned yet, did you? That new alien flick?"

She had seen it, and the two spent the next half hour discussing all the nuances of the independent sci-fi movie and its commentary on the current civil rights issues plaguing the globe. They discussed the composition of the shots and the lighting, but Mary was most interested in the writing and how subtle, natural lines came laden with layers of meaning and suggestion. Eventually, she had to leave, citing a "preexisting appointment with her mother to shop for spring fashions" (she actually did word it like that), so George went back to work.

Thankful that his boss was absent and thereby oblivious to his lengthy break, George completed the remaining hour of his shift invigorated by the conversation. As he was clearing plates and taking orders for greasy pancakes and buttery fried eggs, he was thinking of points to make in the next conversation with Mary – subtleties in films he had rented from Movie Express that would lure her into further discussions. Loneliness was a pandemic among the residents of Ipswich, but he knew she would appreciate what he had to say, and it felt good to not be entirely alone.

The rest of the day went by quickly. Thankfully, George did not have to deliver pizzas that night, so when his shift was concluded at Angela's, he was free to head back to his apartment. It was a beautiful day that was mild enough to lend itself to a walk through Maudson State Park or a cup of coffee downtown, but George preferred to sink into his overstuffed couch and throw in a DVD. It was starting to get pathetic, but it was comfortable.

After a quick change of clothes to escape the smell of french fries, George crouched down by his TV to look through the various DVDs he had neatly stacked in piles of twenty on the floor. He was halfway up his sixth pile, which brought him to around 110 movies – not a bad collection, but not yet the epic library he was working toward. After a few moments of browsing, he settled on a early nineties horror movie, a genre he generally avoided but couldn't help viewing as near-comedies, satirizing their own existence.

The blue glow of the old tube TV was the only light source in the room, washing over George as he sat paralyzed on the couch, as if it were some alien instrument scanning his mind. He was pondering the details and decision to use bright cherry red liquid for the blood effects when his cellphone rang. It was very unusual for him to get calls unless he was late for work, so he was understandably surprised by the interruption. He quickly paused the movie mid-frame and answered.

"Hello?"

"Hey, George. It's Mike Cassidy. I'm outside you're place. Come let me in." His old high school classmate had a thick Boston accent and had recently returned to town. Though George wouldn't expect Mike to reach out to him for friendship, it wasn't all together unreasonable. Few of their graduating class was left in town, and even though they were never best friends, George and Mike always seemed to get along.

"Oh, geez. Okay... hold on. I'll be right out. Everything's okay, right?"

"Yeah, yeah. Just let me in. It's getting fucking cold out here."

George walked around to his front door, which was actually the basement door of the building and could only be accessed by a stairway leading underground. There was a solitary industrial light bulb on the outside. He slid the bolt open, and a large, heavyset man with greasy black hair, stubble, and a poorly fitting outfit stepped through the doorway and into the apartment.

"Jesus, Mike, you look so different!" George was stunned.

"Yeah, I know. I finally grew up." Mike Cassidy had always been puny, but he was a far cry from his former self. "What are you watching?"

"The Slasher, from the nineties. So, uh, did you just come to hang out, or...?" George wasn't trying to be rude, but the visit surprised him, and he wasn't used to his personal space being invaded.

"Hold your horses, Rutherford. I brought you something... well, an opportunity is a better way to describe it." Cassidy walked over and sat down on the beige couch without being invited to sit. George cringed. He was by no means a beacon of cleanliness, but Mike looked smelly, and that was putting it nicely.

"What do you mean?"

"Take a look at this shit." Mike reached into his pocket with a dirty hand and pulled out a plastic baggy of pills. "This is prime. Real Grade A stuff here." He handled the bag carefully, like it was fragile.

"Dude, is that E? You know I'm not into that stuff." George was telling the truth. He didn't do drugs, but he wasn't vehemently against them either. He just found them to be a waste of a money, something overhyped for the limited amount of entertainment he got when tried them. He experimented while he was in New York, and the bitter disappointment of his failure there was forever linked to all aspects of the lifestyle that sent him crawling back to Ipswich.

"Yeah, man, that's cool. I don't care whether you do the shit or not. I brought it for you to sell."

"I dunno..." George had never given thought to such an idea. He truly didn't know how he felt about the proposition. On the one hand, he would be making money that would allow him to work less hours at the McJobs he currently held. On the other, he would be getting into the gritty underbelly of suburban society and risk getting in trouble with the law.

"You could do it for a bit and then use the money to go back out to New York. You are trying to get back there, aren't you? That's what Meg O'Connelly told me. I just need someone in the area until my usual guy gets back from his month on the west coast."

A bell went off in George's head. Quick money to go back would allow him to make up for this wasted time. He could get his life back on track just by selling a little mind candy to the local high school students. It was all starting to make sense to him.

"Just let me think about it for a bit." His conscious told

him not to go through with it, but the allure of money hung in his head like the aroma of a freshly baked pie. Despite how unhealthy it was, it became simply irresistible.

"All right, man, that's what I wanted to hear. I knew you'd be up for it. I told myself 'Mike, that George Rutherford's a solid guy, you'll be able to rely on him.'" He pulled out a joint and lit up.

Meanwhile, George's mind turned over the offer that had been presented. It could be his chance to get back the life he wanted, if only he was first willing to take a step into the dangers of the night. He thought and thought until his brain would think no more, and the two drifted off into the hazy bliss.

Mary

Her limbs were not moving properly, her mouth filled with cotton when she tried to speak. Social situations paralyzed her like the token weakness of a superhero, suddenly and completely. Breathe, Mary told herself. It's okay, it's just George. She wasn't used to boys talking to her, let alone sitting down and joining her for a meal. Her mind began to race as she considered his possible motives. She was sure he wasn't just making fun of her like she suspected others might. Perhaps he genuinely wanted to talk with her. She wondered if it was a date she was having, unsure of the social rules of the situation. Sure, George was almost ten years older than her, but he was still sort of handsome. His messy blond hair and light brown eyes were often emotionless, but when he got excited about a film or novel, he lit up with the excitement of a puppy chasing a ball for the first time.

The two sat in Angela's Diner and talked for what seemed like hours, though it was really only a matter of minutes. The smell of lard and starch filled the air, while the muffins and danishes slowly rotated in their plastic display case, casting a twinkle of light across the room like a halfhearted disco ball. They discussed the latest science fiction movie to hit the theaters and all the subtleties and thematic plot devices they had noticed. It was very intellectually stimulating, and Mary thought George was a fine boy – a fine man.

"So, what did you think of the fact that he was making her roses at the end of it?" George inquired.

"It was cheesy, but I thought it was fitting and completed the movie, unlike other originals where they leave gaping plot holes only to be filled in by the sequel they intend to make, trying to turn everything into a franchise." She was passionate about this subject in particular. Mary hated the idea of film makers selling out. George looked at his watch. Just then she realized she had to leave, and she told George that she was going shopping with her mother. He said he needed to leave as well.

"Crap! I'm sorry, but I have to get back to work. I've used fifteen minutes more of my break that I was supposed to." George smiled as he pushed his chair back and hurried back to the his dirty tables.

After George got up to return to his duties, Mary gathered

her things and left, trying to leave as little of a mess at her table as possible. She wiped her plate with her napkin, which she then neatly folded and placed under the raised ridge of the plate. Her utensils, though used, were licked clean and placed in the spots where she had found them when she sat down. Her cleanliness would show George that she appreciated the conversation, as he wouldn't have as much work to do because of her thoughtfulness. She was worried it could be considered too bold, but she went forth and left a clean table anyway. After packing away the letter she had received from her deadbeat father into her current book of choice and placing it into her backpack, she stood and left.

Outside, it was a mild day, one of those freakish New England Januaries that went from thirty to sixty degrees in the blink of an eye. She could have even gone without her jacket, but she figured it was better to be safe than to be sorry. Since it was so nice, she decided to talk a bit of a longer route back to her house on the southside. Heading down State Street, she passed the turnoff into her neighborhood and started walking toward Maudson State Park. The plants lining the sidewalk were weary with the changes in weather, and those that had any remaining greenery were withering and soggy. It was one of those days that teased you with a warm breeze, bringing forth memories of springtime and jacketless weather, yet if you were to actually make the mistake of wearing the clothes the weather tempted you to wear, it would immediately begin to sleet as the weather gods stuck their tounges out and laughed at your expense. It was an enjoyable walk nevertheless, and Mary loved the inspiration nature gave her for her stories. Still, she regretted that it was not nice enough to sit out in her back yard or in a park downtown to enjoy a good book or fan fiction novel.

As she was walking next to the edge of a dense wood that made up the back yards of an older southside development, she heard a cracking of branches through the trees. She peered through the brambles to see what was causing the noise, hoping to spot a doe or coyote. The rustling stopped suddenly, and from out of the woods and onto the sidewalk stepped a shaggy haired boy, about her age. She had seen him around before but did not know who he was. He wore a pale shirt and brown vest atop somewhat baggy khaki colored trousers that cut off midway down the calves. His eyes were as blue as the summertime sky, and his cheekbones were pronounced and slightly rosy. Mary struggled to catch her breath at the sight of him. She even got nervous around George, and as cute as he was, he had nothing on this newcomer. The boy beamed back.

"Hello, stranger." His voice was pure and honest, boyish but confident, masculine, and intelligent at the same time. "Could I bother you to show me the way back into town? I'm new here, and I seem to be lost."

"Uh… okay." She struggled to get the words out and tried (unsuccessfully) not to look at the boy. "I'm Mary."

"Pleased to make your acquaintance, Mary. I'm Perran." The boy walked with such ease. He seemed completely and entirely comfortable with himself. "I don't know how I ended up coming all the way down here, but I started at Angela's Diner earlier and am looking for Bean, the coffee shop downtown."

"Okay." Mary truly wanted to say more, but she was physically unable to generate sentences in her mind. She considered commenting on his unusual name but decided to stay silent. A gentle breeze of comfortable temperature lazily passed through, rustling the dead foliage on the surrounding ground.

"You aren't very talkative."

"Sorry."

"Say, whose words are those in your arm?" The mysterious boy gestured to the book she was carrying. It was the latest in her favorite series, a group of books she loved so much she couldn't read anything else until she had caught up with what was happening in that particular magical world. Each book in the series amounted to almost 1,000 pages, but Mary breezed through most of them in less than a week.

"Uh... " She was embarrassed. This guy looks like a movie star and is trying to talk to me, and the first thing he notices is that. As much as Mary loved the epic ten-volume fantasy series, she didn't like admitting it to anyone — cute boys least of all. Just my luck, she thought.

The boy looked at her quizzically, cocking his head slightly to the side and smirking to reveal two rows or perfectly white, perfectly aligned teeth. A mischievous look swept across his face, as if he was struck instantly with some devilish idea.

"You should work on your skills of conversation, Mary Augustine." She hadn't mentioned her last name, so this immediately struck her as odd. "And I think I'll be taking that." The boy swept in and pecked Mary on the cheek, rendering her inert. She couldn't have budged a finger if the Earth had cracked open at her feet and the devil himself threatened to engulf her if she would not move. Even then, she probably would still be too stunned, and that was to say nothing of the numb feeling spreading from where he had made contact. Taking advantage of the moment, the shaggy haired knave swiped the book from Mary's hand and bounded off down the street, looking back only once to playfully smile at her as if to say "It's all in good fun, my dear!"

Still stunned, Mary only stared. Right before he turned the bend, she noticed his spotless feet atop the muddy sidewalk. He wasn't wearing any shoes, yet he seemed to be completely comfortable and strangely clean. He turned the corner to leave Mary alone on the sidewalk.

When he was out of sight, she finally regained locomotion in her extremities and absentmindedly pulled her hand up to her cheek to where he had kissed her. It was her first kiss. She could still feel it tingling and wondered in all seriousness if she was glowing. She definitely hadn't imagined it happening like that. She had imagined all types of scenarios from the cheesy to the mundane, but most certainly not that.

Taking her first step, her knees felt rubbery, but with each step following, she felt a bit more powerful. By the time she arrived back at her house, she felt empowered like she never had before. She was desirable! Invincible! She hadn't yet learned the skills of conversing like her contemporaries, nor had she made any progress with her unthinkable idea to flirt with George, but she suddenly felt like anything was possible. She had started the day at her normal junction of inadequacy and complacency and turned the bend toward hope.

Gavin

Gavin Prior was out for a walk during his lunch break when his pager vibrated violently against his belt buckle. Code 465. Another temp had tried to access a non-professional website. At any other firm, the computer would just block the access and display a blank webpage. Of course, at MediCom, the health care communications firm Gavin worked for, the server would go berserk and freeze up if such a request was made. He was the only one who could fix such a problem, so he was forced to cut his lunch break half an hour short. Gavin was Systems Administrator, a humble position in the grand scheme of things, but he worked hard and made a respectable living.

When his brother and wife were tragically lost to the car

accident years ago, Gavin buried his emotion by dedicating himself to his career and to the success of his son Tanner. The day consisted of working, reading the news paper or trade journals to improve his skills, and encouraging his son to excel in his natural gift of athletics. It was the same every day; even the weekends were mostly spent mastering online tutorials of the latest server software that his company would be adopting. He completed the tutorial for the latest release four separate times. All that was about to change, of course.

After successfully fixing the error with the server's frozen internet connection (thanks to the temp who had tried to access obviously inappropriate material and had dramatically exited with a flourish of hand-waving and carefully chosen curse words), Gavin spent the rest of the day updating software packages. It was rather droll, but he didn't mind, and the day went by quickly.

On his way out of the office, Gavin passed many of his coworkers. They nodded in recognition, but he had never taken the time to learn their names or connect with them. He simply was uninterested in making new connections unless they involved USB ports and was borderline incapable. His emotional barriers after the loss of his family were fortified and strong, and it would take a miracle or work of magic to break them down.

Gavin drove his 2001 Passat out of the industrial park and back into town. Driving always made him nervous. The conditions of his brother's and wife's unbelievable fate had been alcohol related. His brother had drank himself into oblivion, convinced his sister-in-law that he was sober, and then driven them both off a bridge en route to the grocery store. With such a freak occurence, it shouldn't have occured to Gavin that he could fall into a similar fate, especially since he very rarely drank or even drove down dangerous roads. Nevertheless, he couldn't help but tense up whenever he was behind the wheel. The irrational fear was even worse when he had to ride with other drivers, though that was a rare occasion at best.

He had some time before Tanner would return from his friend's house and decided to take one of his rare trips to Bean, the downtown coffee shop. Even for someone as reclusive as Gavin, a change of scenery was nice, and he enjoyed sitting by the fireplace and looking out on the water with a quad espresso and the newspaper.

As he entered the brick building that was so typical of downtown Ipswich, a bell rang somewhere in the back of the store. Todd and Colleen, the eccentric owners of Bean, walked out from the back room, laughing with each other about some joke that probably would have gone over Gavin's head. They annoyed him a bit. He was convinced no one could naturally have that much fun with one another.

Gavin walked up and ordered his usual at the antique register that Todd operated with ease.

"Carol! Quad espresso!" he called back to his wife. Gavin was confused, for he always thought the woman's name was Colleen. He was sure of it. Embarrassed that he might have been addressing her incorrectly all this time, he felt obliged to inquire.

"I'm sorry, but I thought your wife's name was Colleen." He looked apologetic. Todd smiled.

"Oh, well yes, but Carol is her rap name." The shopkeeper acted as if this was a completely acceptable explanation.

"Oh." Gavin could have gone further. He could have asked why she had a rap name, why the two were always laughing, or for explanations of the jokes he never understood, but the idea was incredibly unappealing. He concluded they must be hippies, quite possibly high on drugs. He just wanted his espresso and to read his newspaper in peace.

As he collected his drink from the barista station, he heard the bell ring again in the back of the store and looked toward the entrance. Laura Augustine, a woman he vaguely knew from years past, entered the shop. She was a fine looking woman, Gavin noted, but he would never talk to her. She was wearing a fashionable coat with a green and white floral print, modernized with bold lines and thick solid color pockets. For a moment Gavin considered how youthfully beautiful she looked for a woman in her forties, but quickly shrugged it off. Though he was capable of finding other women attractive, he simply couldn't be bothered to put the effort in. Change was unfamiliar, and Gavin's routine and simple life was extremely comfortable.

Walking over to his favorite chair, he noticed that a shaggy haired boy he had never seen in town before was sitting in the seat directly across from him reading what appeared to be a very old book with pages yellowed with age. Gavin also noticed that the boy wasn't wearing any shoes, which was undoubtedly a health violation, though he didn't want to put up a fuss. He simply sat down in his favorite high-back chair that was angled perfectly to offer a simultaneous view of both the fireplace and the Merrimack and began to sip his drink. Every once in a while, he would look from his newspaper over to where Laura Augustine was sitting across the room, just to take in the sight of her. After one such glance, he saw that the strange shoeless boy was watching him with a knowing smirk. Smug bastard. Feeling embarrassed, Gavin became very intent on keeping his concentration on the newspaper.

Several minutes later, the boy sitting across from him rose to leave, leaving his book on the chair which he had been occupying. He passed very closely by Gavin and accidentally brushed against his shoulder as he did. He looked back as he continued to walk and smiled.

"Many apologies, friend," he said melodically. Gavin found the stranger to be unnerving but didn't say anything and merely grunted in reply, wordlessly acknowledging the apology. He turned back to his newspaper and looked for the story regarding sidewalk preservation that the front page had advertised was hidden in one of the inner sections. After a few moments of searching, he became frustrated and looked back out the window. It was a beautiful winter day.

Suddenly, and without warning, Gavin felt an inner warmth spreading across his body, starting at his fingertips. Within seconds, he found himself smiling uncontrollably. All the world around him had a strange sparkle like he had never seen before. He noted how beautiful his surroundings were and was grateful he could experience them. The chair he was sitting it was unbelievable comfortable, and he considered how masterfully it was constructed. The windows looking out onto the river spread the light into a thousand individual beams, each landing in a unique spot and glowing like the sun.

He knew something very strange was happening to him but he didn't mind. He still had complete control, and the odd sensation was very comforting anyway. Looking over at Laura once again with a renewed confidence, he saw she was practically glowing with beauty. Her lips were full and red, her cheeks naturally pink, her eyes as green as Christmas tree needles. Her hair fell in locks down her head, each bobbing with the movement of her body, dancing with her walk. She emitted a quiet confidence and kindness, an understanding and caring that he inexplicably knew was often buried but had given him the privilege of observing for one of its rare emergences into the world of others. Instantly, he knew he had to conquer his insecurities and win her heart. He didn't know where the thought came from, but he knew it to be unquestionably true and had no will to doubt it. He knew he couldn't be happy unless he won her heart. So beautiful was his lover, his nymph. That was the moment that the man who never spoke, who spent the entirety of his days neglecting all other human beings, fell deeply and irrevocably in love.

PART TWO

Tanner and Timothy

Tanner opened the door to his home and entered the parlor, his friend Timothy in tow. They sprawled out on the couch, and Tanner clicked on the flat panel television, flipping it immediately to MTV where a trashy faux reality show was currently concluding. The young bachelor was just about to choose which of the grandmas to date for a $1,000 cash prize.

"What did you think of Ricky's new rig?" Timothy asked, referring to the new home theater setup their friend had showed them that day. He reached over to the lone candy bowl on the side table that no one besides him ever touched.

"It was pretty epic, but I think a PlayStation would have looked better on it. They have the best graphics on high def

TVs." Tanner started rustling through his pockets looking for his cellphone. "Hey, man, have you seen my phone?"

"No, I don't think so." As soon as he said it, Timothy spotted it in a dent in the couch where he sat and snatched it up. "Oh, you mean THIS phone?" He started hitting the screen to make it look like he was snooping through the text messages.

"Cut it out, Timothy! Give it back." Tanner was stern but not unkind, and there was an air of playfullness in his tone. Timothy was, after all, his best friend.

"Geez, fine. Take it, homo." The insult didn't sound right coming from Timothy. He was too nice, and Tanner could always tell when he was forcing an insult or a curse word to fit the social expectations of teenage vernacular. His green eyes perpetually betrayed his anger. They were always kind. It came out as more of a "Take it... h-homo" than anything else. Tanner never acknowledged his lack of insulting ability, it made him smile inside that he had such a kindhearted friend. Timothy tossed the phone over to Tanner on the other end of the couch. It was a new touchscreen phone without a single button. Timothy's phone was four years old. Such is life.

"Boys, dinner's ready!" Gavin called from the kitchen. The boys stopped in their tracks and looked at each other, confused. Tanner's father never cooked – ever. This was weird. They slowly got up and walked into the kitchen hesitantly to find a chicken dish with a deliciously aromatic mustard sauce and grapes waiting for them at the table. It almost looked gourmet, presented on a bed of risotto with with a parsley sprig border. Again, they glanced at each other in sheer amazement. There was even a bottle of merlot.

"What's up with all this, Dad?" Tanner considered the possibility that his father had gotten a promotion, though he wasn't aware there were any higher positions in the IT department where he worked.

"What do you mean? Can't I make a nice meal for dinner?" Gavin chuckled to himself and began to load his plate with risotto and chicken.

"I guess so." Tanner decided to just leave it alone. He wasn't sure what was going on, but if something was up, his father would tell him eventually, in his own way. The Priors didn't do family talks or confrontation. It was just too awkward. Besides, everything looked delicious, so who was he to complain or question.

"So, where were you two?" Gavin passed the plate down to Timothy. Now, he was serving plates for the boys as well? Something was definitely off. Still, the two boys decided to go with the flow and, shrugging their shoulders, passed the plates along. It all looked so delicious, something Timothy in particular was very unused to.

"We were over at Ricky's house. His parents just bought him a new high def flat screen that looks awesome with his XBox." They started to eat, but Timothy kept glancing over at Tanner, whose jawline was particularly defined and accentuated by the lighting in the kitchen. The glances went unnoticed.

"That sounds like fun." Gavin took a bite of his chicken and continued while still chewing, "You boys wouldn't happen to know the Augustine girl, would you? I think her name is Mary." He tried to look casual, but it came off a bit too excited. Still, it was lumped with his other odd behavior and went ignored.

"I don't know her, but I've seen her around town. She's kinda weird." Tanner said, looking over to Timothy for back up. "Right, Timothy?"

"Yeah, I guess so. I'm not sure I even know who she is, but if I'm thinking of the right girl, then she is pretty strange."

"You shouldn't say things like that. I'm sure she's perfectly nice, and if she takes after her mother, she's probably a looker. Why don't you ask her out on a date, Tanner? You are going to graduate soon, and you're a star athlete, but I haven't seen you out with anyone." Gavin had never considered the fact that his son didn't have a girlfriend at his age. He had always been too concerned about the boy's athletic standing to pay attention to his social life. He made a mental note to encourage his son to date more often.

"Yeah, maybe." Tanner looked down at his dinner and picked nonchalantly at the pieces of chicken that were left. He was clearly unsettled by his father's weird behavior. His father finished his dinner and got up to take his plate to the sink, leaving the boys alone at the table. Timothy could sense something was up. Just as Gavin smiled and bid the two boys a good night, a wave of hormonal frustration hit Tanner like a freight train square on the head.

Teenage hormones are an odd entity. The day could be bright and perfect, but if the illusive hormonal army decided to lay seige on the teenage emotions, it can be a Jekyll and Hyde transformation. Without explanation, frustration can render an otherwise intelligent teenager unable to communicate or reason. Worse than a grouchy mother bear interrupted from her meal and guarding her cubs from a perceived threat, a hormonal teenager is a force to be reckoned with. And in this precise moment, such was Tanner.

"Hey, Tanner, why don't you stay over at my place tonight?" Timothy offered, thinking Tanner might want to get out of the house for once – particularly with his dad acting so weird. Despite his attendance at Saint Andrews, Timothy's house was on the southside of town. He had a very dysfunctional family, and every time Tanner had stopped by on the way to practice or after a game, Timothy's parents had been in some stage of a screaming argument. The house wasn't a trash heap, but it most certainly wasn't clean or appealing either. Timothy was unaware that the hormonal plague had infiltrated his friend's emotions already.

"Why don't I just sleep at the dump?" Too harsh. Tanner didn't care though. There was something about his father's behavior that had put him in a foul mood. He wasn't sure why.

"Shit, Tanner, that was uncalled for." Timothy was shocked at the blatant insult from his supposed best friend.

"Yeah, well maybe you should have thought about it first." He wasn't even making much sense any longer. His mind was clearly somewhere else, drifting among his angry thoughts and frustrations.

"Jesus, what the hell did I do to you? I was just trying to be nice. Enjoy your fucking dinner." Timothy pushed the seat out from under himself so violently that it toppled over onto the Italian tile floor. He grabbed his coat off the couch on his way past and slammed the front door in his wake. Tanner just sat at the dinner table, fuming. He didn't know why an innocent invitation bothered him so much or why he had suddenly felt so much hostility toward his best friend. His father's change in personality could have been the cause, or maybe it was just that his normal routine was so suddenly interrupted. Something was wrong, even if he didn't know what it was.

He finished his plate and slammed it into the sink, a small piece chipping off as it landed. The cleaning lady that came during the day wasn't technically required to do the dishes, but he couldn't be bothered. He was too inexplicably pissed off. He exhaled loudly and stomped up the narrow staircases to his attic bedroom. Throwing the door open with unneccessary force, he turned off his light immediately and walked to the center of the room. With dramatic force, he ripped his clothes off and jumped into his bed, staring up at the exposed ceiling beams.

The frustration churned inside of him, tearing up the walls of his insides. He wished only to understand why it was there. He could think of no probable explanation. There were no logical reasons for it. His paintings left untouched for the night, he lay there letting the glow of streetlights dance across his conflicted teenage self before succumbing to a sleep he had to convince himself was dreamless the next day, though in actuality, it was filled with a truth too difficult for him to face alone.

Mary and Laura

Even floating among the clouds would not cause Mary to feel as exhilirated as she had on her walk home. She was a woman now, and she felt inspired. Good stories would flow tonight because of this. She would composes her masterwork of romance and love and extravagent gala dinners and, of course, kissing. She had received her first kiss. It was official.

The walk home took less time than expected, and before she knew it, she was unlocking the front door of her house and walking into the living room. She flopped down on the couch and sighed, looking up at the ceiling with a smile on her face. The strange boy was so handsome and unquenchably alluring. She visualized their first date, engagement, wedding day, and anniversaries to come.

His shaggy hair would be trimmed shorter, but not too short, for it was uncharacteristic of him to go too short. It would be just right – like Mr. Darcy's, perhaps. Perfectly styled, his dark hair would frame his light eyes, and he would be wearing a tuxedo with black bowtie. She would be in the most gorgeous of all wedding gowns, accentuating her figure and flowing gracefully to the ground like liquid, pooling as her train dragged behind her like a shallow river endlessly cascading over its pebbly bed. The sea breeze would wash over them (for they would naturally be in Hawaii or the Caribbean), and they would go barefoot on the sand as the sun set and they recited their vows. Only their closest family would attend. And this is where Mary she got stuck. Granted, she didn't know the boy, but for the life of her should couldn't even imagine his family, ficticious or otherwise. He was so strangely confident and independent.

She let her fantasy take the reigns and allowed her mind to wander for a while. Eventually, she rose from the couch and went up to her room, where she opened her word processor and started on a new story. She outlined a romantic epic, modelling the heroine after herself and the mysterious lover after her newly discovered paramour. The typing was melodic to her, and she continued without pause for nearly an hour. When she was finished with her outline, she reread it and realized she knew nothing about the boy that had bestowed womanhood upon her. The more she contemplated the situation, the closer she came to realizing that she did not really love Perran, but rather was in love with the new world presented to her. She laughed in spite of herself – her, of all people, getting carried away by teenage romance. Upon this realization, she clicked delete on the the story outline and sighed. It had been a nice fantasy and left her sane and still in a wonderful mood. She went back downstairs, gathering her thoughts and returning to regular activity. Still, she was peaceful and serene as she pulled out the books she needed to start her homework.

Her Spanish workbook waited in the murky shadows of her backpack, taunting her with its difficult concepts. She dreaded the personal 'a' and the subjunctive conjugation exercises she would be forced to complete. Her mood allowed her to delve into the confines of her backpack and retrieve the book with confidence. She might not be the best, but goddammit, she was going to get a passing grade on her assignment. If she had any luck, her fantastical mind would lend itself well to great new stories, and she could leave academia behind forever, become the American J.K. Rowling, and live off her fortunes in her fantasy world till the sun set on her story. Presently, she decided to start with her homework and leave her lifetime achievements for later.

As she started on her English paper an hour later, carefully scribbling notes in the pillar outline her teacher provided her with, her mother walked in from the back door.

"Anyone home?" she called out to the house.

"I'm in here, Mom!" Mary was sitting on the floor doing her work on the living room coffee table, materials spread out in a circle around her. Laura walked into the room with her half finished cappuccino in a takeout cup from Bean. Mary noticed at once.

"Ooh, did you get me any tea?" she asked excitedly. The tea selection at Bean consisted of Mary's absolute favorite beverages, which her mother knew, specifically the yerba matte latte with honey and vanilla added in.

"No, I forgot," Laura said without regret as she walked over to the liquor cabinet to retrieve the night's spirits of choice, dragonberry Bacardi.

"Mom, you know it's my favorite. It can't be more than three dollars!" Mary rarely went to Bean herself, as the social rules of talking with people she ran into downtown (and she always ran into people) were complicated and foreign territory for her.

"I'm sorry, Mary. I just forgot." Laura was annoyed with being pestered. She had had a long day. Mary was used to her mother's temperamental moods and decided with little tact to change the subject.

"I got a letter from Dad."

Silence.

She struggled to recover from the faux pas.

"He's not visiting or anything. Just wanted to check in. He apologized for not writing. Said he was busy." She spoke quickly. "Apparently, he moved to New York City. He said something about being an agent for young reality show actresses."

There was an uncomfortable pause and then, "Oh, and why am I not surprised?" Laura was trying to keep herself together, but the battle had resumed. Whenever she thought of her ex-husband, there was a clash of the titans within her heart. Half of her was absolutely disgusted at the treatment she received from him, while the other half wanted nothing but to have him back at any cost or humiliation. The desire for his return generally won out, especially when there were booze around to drown out her reasonable sensibilities.

Mary, on the other hand, didn't really care one way or the other. She had mourned the loss of her father already, and his sudden communication couldn't mean less to her. She had determined that if he ever showed up again, she would be civil to him. The man was her father, after all. But beyond that, he was no longer a part of her life.

"Do you mind if I take a look at the letter?" There was desperation in her eyes.

Mary started digging through her backpack, but came up empty handed. "Shoot. I know I put it in here somewhere. It has to be here. I hope it didn't fall out." After several minutes of looking, however, she gave up. "It must be in my room somewhere with my stories." Both Mary and Laura knew that if this was the case, there was very little chance of finding it anytime in the near future. They both sighed, and Laura fixed herself a drink as Mary returned to her schoolwork.

There was a time when Laura didn't feel the need to drink away her memories. She thought of this as she glanced at the family photos hanging on the walls, almost all of them from before Joseph left. Her favorite was family picture from their vacation in Vermont at Lake Champlain. Mary was just a young girl, perfectly content to play among the small waves that quietly lapped against the shore. Every time a wave found such fortune as to properly break against the rocky sand, she would clap her hands and shriek with glee, smiling as if nothing in the world could be more exciting.

Joseph and Laura sat on beach chairs watching their young daughter, marvelling at her innocence. Every couple of minutes, Joe would go and join his daughter and play with her in the water, getting down on his knees to join her at eye level and revel in the simply joys of childhood. Laura watched on and fell for her husband for what seemed like the thousandth time as his emotional side crept out from the shadows. This is the real Joseph Augustine, she told herself. This is the man I love. He would return to her and peck her on the cheek before sitting down again and staring out at the water.

It was shortly after one of his play sessions with Mary that Joseph presented a small bouquet of lilacs (Laura's favorite flower) with a card professing his continuing love for his wife. He had ducked away quietly to gather them in a nearby cottage garden while his wife lounged in the sun, a clever romantic if there ever was one. It was a small gesture, sure, but it was so undeniably romantic that it made Laura feel more desired than she had in years. The emotions that started to expand inside felt like they could sustain her for a lifetime.

That memory was Laura's favorite, but it was her curse. The heartbreaking and unfortunate truth was that Joseph Augustine had peaked at that moment. Never again would Laura receive flowers and a card or see her husband play with his daughter in the sand. Thereafter, she would consider herself lucky when he was courteous enough to help with the dishes or consider her enjoyment in their afterhours activities.

It wasn't long before Joseph willingly handed his self-control over to alcohol, followed quickly by drugs – the kind that involve a knack for chemistry. And from there, the Augustines' family life went to the dogs. For four more years, they coexisted, albeit dysfunctionally. Joseph would either yell or become fused with the couch in some form of substance induced paralysis. Laura began to drink as well, though not to the point of alcoholism. Young Mary knew her life wasn't exactly Leave it to Beaver, but she didn't know the extent of the problems either. They never yelled in front of her, and the worst abuse she ever received was a strong helping of neglect.

Yet despite all this, the scent of the lilacs lingered in Laura's memory. The knowledge that Joseph was capable of it ate her up, and she repeatedly told herself they could get return to that, that they could fix things. Joseph left Laura and Mary alone to fend for themselves as he went off to chase young girls barely above Los Angeles jailbait age, yet Laura still clung to this memory, hit the bottle harder than ever, and hoped that somehow, through some romantic miracle worthy of a Lifetime movie, things could return to how they were.

And so it was that while Mary halfheartedly worked on her assignments so that she could someday achieve her fantasy, Laura needed more than magic to let go of her own.

George and Mary

Stepping out of his apartment, George was greeted with one of the most hopeful messages Mother Nature was known to give: winter was breaking. Gone were the days of frigid cold that made the inside of his nostrils feel like frozen canyons caked with ice, the days that turned his fingers into useless vegetables, more prosthetic than actual extremity, and the days that made the top of his cheeks just under the eye burn with frostbite. The snow that had been lingering throughout all of March had finally melted, and the sun was hanging alone in a genuinely blue sky, lacking any of the characteristic winter grey.

He looked around suspiciously, his paranoia on high alert since he had decided to take Mike Cassidy up on his business proposition. At first, he was conflicted and decided to pass on the offer, being all too nervous about its legal implications. It was one of his regular nights watching television, but a commercial for a new movie about artists dwelling in New York City filled the screen and caught his attention. Enormous bohemian lofts inhabited by mid-twenties bombshells hanging on floppy haired hipsters passed across his screen while the latest indie music erupted from his surround sound speakers, taunting him. In that moment, tied up in the glamorous lifestyle that he knew could be his, he picked up his phone and dialed Mike.

"That offer that you made? I'll do it," he had said, sealing his fate to miniature Ziploc baggies and meetings masked in darkness.

In recent months, George had found the financial success Mike spoke of and come into fortune (relatively speaking, of course) through the business opportunity that landed on his doorstep. He likened it to the mythical stork leaving a baby at a deserving family's door, except that the stork was a scary large man, and the baby was roughly $5,000 cash. Granted, most of that had to be repaid for materials and the bill of his untraceable cellphone, but there was still upwards of $1,000 in profit that he was able to use for himself. For the most part, life was the same though.

He had so far resisted any temptations to fall into destructive habits and was very minimally involved in the world he dealt with (and to) on a regular basis. Customers were visited at a public location of their choosing and never received George's real phone number, address, or name. He was careful to the point of paranoia, which he found necessary, considering the wares he happened to be pushing.

His new financial freedom had allowed him to quit his

nighttime pizza delivery job, though he kept his job at Angela's Diner for the social contact and exposure to the community. His favorite activity continued to be movies in his basement apartment, but like every other human, George needed some form of contact with others that transcended the forced awkwardness of an illegal drug transaction.

George wandered slowly toward Movie Express, which was housed in the Tannery, a converted mill in downtown Ipswich that was now home to several local businesses. He would sometimes spend upwards of thirty minutes browsing the titles at the video rental store, despite already having a fairly good sense of the existing inventory. Mary Augustine generally provided good conversation and was really starting to open up in recent months. Her socially awkward nature was beginning to melt away, something he had noticed several months before. He wasn't sure why she was changing, but he was glad to see it.

The first thing he noticed during his prior visit was that she was not reading when he entered the store. She had always been reading whenever he saw her, so he inquired as to why she was without a book that day. She answered that the book she was reading was stolen, and she couldn't continue until she bought another copy of the almost impossible to find volume. It was because she had nothing to read that she was forced to make conversation with George, and they both discovered a mutual interest in fan made movies and sequels. Granted, they had talked about films and literature before, but this conversation was somehow different. Mary had opened up about a passion, and it was clear that she was sharing her true joy for the art form without any restraint or hesitation. She was growing, it seemed.

Presently, George walked into the Movie Express plaza; itself a remnant of the early mills of the Merrimack with large wooden beams and brick walls, some removed and replaced with trendy plate glass windows to give it a modern look without being abstract. There were a few cars in the parking lot and two boys talking outside the store. They clearly didn't want people noticing them, and despite recognizing one of them, George slipped into the rental store quickly without approaching. Looking over to the side, he saw Mary behind the counter changing the DVD that played on the old CRT televisions mounted to the walls throughout the store. She was wearing a fashionable red and white fitted shirt, something out of character for her but very becoming.

"Afternoon, Mary!" George called over as he began to browse the new releases at the section labeled 'A.'

"Hi, George. Hey, how was that oldie you rented the other day – the one with the impossible-to-pronounce title?"

"Oh, you mean Ninotchka? It was really good. Kept my attention and actually made me laugh, which is harder with old humor."

"Glad to hear it. What are you looking for today?" She pressed play, and the FBI warning that was never read by a single human being appeared simultaneously on the many old screens across the room. Just seeing the FBI logo surround him made George shiver. He shook it off.

"Nothing special. Just something for tonight."

"What about the new Tarantino film?" Mary noticed George's kind, inquisitive eyes as he browsed the different titles. So welcoming. His dirty blonde floppy hair unintentionally fell onto his face, and he brushed it away playfully. He was boyish and cute, she thought, despite the fact that he was fast approaching his late twenties.

"I heard it wasn't that great?" He made it sound like a question.

"George Rutherford, since when do you listen to reviews?" Mary considered addressing him by his full name might be too flirty – not that she wanted to flirt with George, right?

"I suppose you're right. Hmm..." George walked through all the aisles of the store, pausing here and there to read the back of a DVD case before moving on to the next section.

He browsed in silence, the only noise coming from the low volume of the TVs playing one of the latest releases, enticing potential customers to rent it. Mary was just starting to catalog missing rentals when the bell attached to the front door announced a new customer, and she saw the light eyed knave walk in.

"Good afternoon, Mary." Perran smiled as he approached. Mary could not get over his perfect teeth.

"Hello." She was no longer struck inert by his presence but somewhat resented the book theft and violation of the kiss. It was innocent enough, but she still couldn't help but feel perturbed. He didn't seem to notice.

"May I inquire as to whether or not you have The Hand that Make You Fair in your inventory?" Perran leaned against the merchandiser that sat next to the counter and looked entirely at ease. He was shoeless, as usual. Mary typed into the old keyboard, each key clacking like a wooden spoon against a countertop as she searched.

"I'm afraid we don't." She stared him down. He was still rather dashing, thief or not.

"Pity," Perran sighed and looked around the store. Upon spotting George, he raised his eyebrows and smiled. "He came back, I see."

"I'm sorry?" Mary had no idea what the strange boy was talking about.

"No bother, friend. I'll see you around town." He winked, then walked – or almost glided – out out of the store. Only when he was out of sight did Mary notice a single small sunflower on the countertop with a note attached. She pulled it close to her face and read, "My apologies. -P." Maybe he wasn't that bad after all.

George returned to the front of the store with a title unknown to Mary. He smiled at her as he put it on the counter. George was a bit older and anything but perfect, but at least he was genuine. She appreciated that he didn't seem like he had anything to hide, that he made an honest living at Angela's Diner, and that they shared interests and enjoyed each other's company. Ringing up his rental for the day, she smiled a more than friendly smile.

Tanner and Perran

The characteristic soaring ceilings of the buildings Saint Andrews Academy echoed the many footsteps of the hormone ridden teenagers as they traversed the hallways in between classes. Tanner and his fellow teammates joked around with each other as they slowly made their way to the English classroom where they were scheduled to do a worksheet on Oscar Wilde's "Our Town." In the hallway, they passed every cliché private school attendee: the princess imported on her rich Indian father's dime, the new money transplant from Jersey that aspired to have a sixteenth birthday party featured on MTV, the waspy blond fellow who talked of drinking pelligrino on his father's sailboat while listening to Euro pop. All of them were present in the hallowed halls of education. Tanner found it incessantly irritating.

The weather was starting to warm up to the idea of facilitating a proper spring, and Tanner's soccer teammates were discussing a pickup game after English, which was their last class that day. It was agreed, with enthusiastic whoops all around, minus Timothy who had never really opened entirely back up since his spat with Tanner months before. Tanner just wanted to have his best friend back in his full capacity. He wanted to see his eyes light up when he suggested they hang out after school or smirk at him when he made a lame joke. They were talking again, but their conversations almost always included an uncomfortable silence where they would search each other's eyes for the answer. As of yet, they were still searching, wondering why the other one was bothered so much by a situation that didn't even have a clear conflict – or rather, a situation that didn't have a clear conflict that they were willing to admit.

Tanner playfully punched the team goalie, Ricky Gervez, in the arm as they sauntered into Ms. Ramsay's English classroom. The unusual instructor had recently decorated the room with red velvet curtains sporting shiny golden ropes that tied to hooks in the wall on either side of the windows. Tanner noticed how the colors tied in perfectly to the brownish red of the brick walls and aged white stone window frames; he made a mental note to try painting the image after he finished his current project.

"Pupils, kindly do me the favor of taking your seats and preparing your materials. Class will begin momentarily," Ms. Ramsay said, her red hair less frizzy than normal today and tied into a long ponytail that extended halfway down her torso. She always spoke as if she were addressing Queen Elizabeth. The new students always gossiped about how weird she was, but seniors like Tanner and his cohorts were seasoned to the unusual quirks of Tabetha Ramsay.

"Before we begin, I would like you to note that we will be having our examination on the works of Mr. Oscar Wilde on the April 24, only a few weeks from now."

Immediately, the announcement was protested, for the first spring season soccer game was the day before the scheduled exam. It was tradition that one of the players would host a house party the night after the first game of a season, so there would undoubtedly be little to no studying going on the day before the important test.

Timothy raised his hand, clearly more polite than shouting his disagreement out of turn.

"Mr. Barber, why all the commotion?" Ms. Ramsay asked him with a dramatic flourish of her hand.

"Ms. R., there is a very important soccer game the night before, and I think my teammates and I are just concerned for our grades if we don't have the proper amount of time to study for your test."

Tanner noticed how handsome Timothy looked as he formally addressed the instructor. No, he didn't. It's just his outfit — yeah, that's it. It's a nice outfit. Or maybe he got a haircut. Handsome was too strong a word. Tanner wasn't sure why he noticed that.

"Ah, I see." Ms. Ramsay walked over to the standalone globe housed in a faux gold frame with poorly molded claw feet. "You all must know that I appreciate your concern of academic standing, but college awaits you in a few short months, and if you do not learn to pace your studying now, failure surely awaits you. An examination cannot be mastered the night before it graces your desk. It must be prepared for over time, with multiple sessions of study. I'm afraid the predetermined date stands." There were a few final moans and groans, but Ricky's halfhearted throw of a crumpled paper was the end of it. They would just have to manage. Such is life, thought Timothy.

"Moving on, if you would all please take of these worksheets and pass them back, we are going to discover which of you came prepared with the assigned reading." Tabetha Ramsay started passing out worksheets that seemingly came from nowhere as the class in its entirety dreaded the instructors inevitable discovery that not a single one of them read the required pages the night before.

The monotonal mechanized chime eventually signalled the end of class, and everyone stood up, creating a simultaneous screech of chairs against the old wooden floors followed by a rustling of nylon backpacks against pique polo shirts. Timothy watched Tanner from behind as he exited the classroom and noticed that sleeves were tighter on his arms than usual. It was probably from soccer workouts starting up again. Neither Timothy nor Tanner noticed that Perran stayed back as everyone left, sitting silently at his desk and staring Ms. Ramsay down with his chilling eyes until all was silent and the class had moved on to their afternoon activities.

Ms. Ramsay appraised Perran and squinted one eye deep in thought. Suddenly, she reached into her desk, pulled out an apple, and gently threw it across the room at Perran's head, all in one graceful and quick motion. The strange boy snatched it in midair, whipped it around his back, switching hands, and bit into it as he manuevered and put his bare feet up on the desk.

"Thought you might be hungry." She smiled. Perran nodded thoughtfully in response. When he had swallowed, he gave his characteristic mischevious smirk.

"Prior?" he cryptically inquired. The sun coming in through the antique windows danced playfully across his messy dark brown hair.

"Oh, I think soccer is his game," the instructor replied, walking over and putting several loose books away on the old bookshelf next to her desk.

"I surmised as much." Perran stood and walked over to the window, looking out onto the campus, readily awaiting spring's promised arrival. The two stood together in silence for several minutes. It was beginning to get warmer out, almost to the point where jackets were no longer necessary. Perran never wore jackets, even in the deepest freeze of winter.

"And Barber?" Ms. Ramsay asked, looking up from her desk where she had started to grade papers.

"Of course I've noticed. We talk." He looked around the room as if he were expecting to spot a great treasure hidden somewhere in plain sight or some sudden inspiration to strike him from the sight of something in the room.

"It's a pleasure to see you again, Perran." There was great affection in her voice.

"Ah, the pleasure is always mine, Tabetha." Perran smiled at the eccentric English instructor and turned toward the door, walking out to fields where some struggling adolescants needed a bit of help. Before the stubborn likes of eighteen-year-olds would ever consider help, though, one needed to earn their respect.

The boys on the Saint Andrews soccer team jeered at each other as they passed the ball around during their pickup game after class. Timothy passed back to Tanner as he was getting blocked in by Ricky and Josh, who were on the opposing side. Tanner was playing midfield, an unusual position for him, and once Timothy was freed up from the previous blockade, he passed back to him. Timothy then went to make a shot against Sam, who was trying out as goalie for the day, and gave the shot some spin to give him a difficult time saving it. Before it could reach the net, Perran Nemerov shot out from the sidelines (no one had seen him standing there) and jumped up over the ball's trajectory, kicking it down to the ground as he passed over it. It came to a complete stop without bouncing or rolling. The team exploded.

"Just what the hell do you think you're doing, nancy boy?" Sam shouted out. "We are playing an effing game here, and you are not invited!"

Perran didn't say anything. He just looked around at the players with his mischevious smirk. A few of the other boys called out vulgar names or orders for him to leave the field. He kept silent until everyone finally just stared, waiting for him to respond. Just as the length of the silence was about to get awkward, he spoke, barely above an audible volume, inspecting his fingernails as he did so.

"Let's play a little game." His eyes lit up.

"If you wanna play, wait till we've finished this one," Timothy suggested, trying to offer a compromise.

"I have the ball. I make the rules." The tension was visible. "I happen to think you guys could use some work, so I figure a little wager was in order."

"Ha, this fucking fairy boy thinks he can outplay us!" Ricky yelled, grabbing his stomach as he mocked surprise.

"What do you mean 'wager?'" Tanner asked, intrigued.

"Well, since I so rudely interrupted your game for my own pleasure, if I win, I'll simply walk away, and your stunned faces will be enough payment."

"And when you lose?" Ricky asked, positive that there could be no other outcome.

"I won't, but if I lose, I happen to possess the answers to Ms. Ramsay's 'Our Town' exam, which I would gladly pass on to you fine gentlemen."

That was all they needed to hear. The entire team knew they were better than this androdginous newcomer, let alone playing ten to one. The exam was as good as aced, and this would allow them to guiltlessly party the night before – guilt being relative, of course.

"Deal." Tanner walked over and took the ball from Perran. "Home team starts."

It was a game like no other. The best of the respected Saint Andrews team was playing, yet one boy alone held the field – and strong. For the first twenty minutes, it was fairly even. Perran had speed like none of the other boys could dream of having, and he wove in and out of the other players like a seasoned professional. To top things off, he was barefoot. At one point in the beginning of the game, he slid feet-first in between the legs of another player as he was running and without missing a beat resumed his erect posture and stole the ball from the player on the other side. His skills were unreal.

Still, he was just one person, and the team scored a couple of goals against him early on. After the first twenty minutes, though, what had seemed to be impossible skills to begin with were dwarfed when he kicked in even more energy and talent. He was flipping over heads and moving the ball with leg movements that seemed impossibly fast and perfectly timed, the kind of moves only possible in movies and videogames. From then on, the team did not score a single goal against him, while he racked up several more points of his own.

"He's cheating!" Tanner yelled out. "That's impossible! No way!"

Perran kept moving like liquid through the other players but locked his eyes on Tanner. As he wove in and out, ducked and jumped, his gaze did not break from Tanner's eyes, except when necessary to assess the position of the ball and other players. The entire time, he had a mischevious smirk on his face. When he finally found an opening, he kicked the ball up into the air in front of him and launched himself off the ground and into a flip. As his legs were coming back up and around, he clobbered the ball with one bare foot and sent it barreling toward Tanner's head.

The girls that had gathered on the sideline could hear a resounding crack as the ball hit Tanner square in the face with unstoppable force. Faster than gravity could have pulled him, he was on the ground writhing, holding his hands to his face as the soccer ball rolled lazily away. Perran appeared before him, looming above and smiling. He had not yet broken a sweat and looked immaculate as ever.

"Sorry, friend. I get carried away sometimes." He extended his hand. "It's just a game, right?"

Tanner just glared. He was panting both from exertion and insurmountable anger. For a moment, Perran didn't move. Realizing Tanner wasn't going to admit defeat in front of a crowd by taking his hand, he pulled it back and looked up at everyone who had circled around them. Addressing no one in particular, he sighed, visibly disappointed, and began to walk toward the woods. "Guess that's that then." His gate was graceful as he walked out of sight.

Tanner was still panting, fury in his eyes.

The crowd dispersed from the circle, and people started to gather their things, everyone mumbling and complaining about the game. Everyone agreed it was unfair, even though they could not articulate a reason as to how they had lost. Timothy approached Tanner and extended his hand, Tanner looked up and caught himself before he let loose the relieved smile that threatened to show itself. Again, he did not know why. The warmth of Timothy's hand was comforting, the calluses intriguing. He held on to the hand one second longer than he should have as he got up, and immediately upon realizing it, he shoved Timothy away.

"What?" Timothy asked, confused, "I was just trying to help you up."

Tanner didn't answer and just walked away, his eye swelling

and growing dark with a bruise. He didn't have an answer. He was confused too.

George and [Censored]

Like a firefly hanging on to the last threads of life, the flourescent bulb flickered against its filthy yellowing protector. The cement stairwell was bathed in a neon glow that seemed to dance with the chirping of the crickets just a few feet away out the open doorway that led to to a untravelled part of Maudson State Park.

George hated stairwells. Why so many of his customers preferred to meet in the abandoned groundskeeping building in the State Park at godawful hours of the night was beyond his reasoning. He supposed it was the last place he would ever imagine Ipswich law enforcement patrolling. Still, he was creeped out and not completely accustomed to the drug trafficking business. In one documentary he recently watched, the SWAT teams that were interviewed referred to staircases as "funnels of death" due to the angle that a shooter could achieve while maximizing their own protection. Funnels of death, just wonderful. He imagined his potential customers, unbeknowst to him, waiting on the upper floor of the building with weapons at the ready, preparing to strike him down and steal his money and their poisons of choice. Still, if he was ever going to make it back to New York, he needed the money and had to take the risk in order to get it. Ipswich was holding on to his ankles and trying to pull him back beneath the surface of the sea of mediocrity, but he still wanted to try and pull himself out and above.

He had so far stayed very careful with his illegal business endeavors, presented to him by the creepy Mike Cassidy. Most importantly to him, he had not let himself give in to the temptation of trying any of the products that he pushed. He knew that if he crossed that line, it would be an express ticket to failure, if not worse.

The most surprising aspect of the new adventure was the revelation of the clientelle. Little did he know that [Censored], the manager at Movie Express was the biggest friend of Mary Jane on the north shore, or so it seemed. Calling him surprised would be an understatement when he learned that [Censored], the dean of [An Academy]'s daughter enjoyed more than a little nose candy on weekends. Such knowledge made him confident, as he was sure they wouldn't want their secrets to get out, and as such would never reveal his identity, as this would mean admitting their struggles. It was his insurance as much as it was his plague. He knew the identities and secrets of people who had a lot to lose, people who might use extreme methods to keep their secrets safe. Needless to say, George had become very jumpy with the stress he was experiencing regarding the whole issue. He was starting to understand why the drugs seemed appealing at times, if only to calm the nerves. For now, he still resisted.

He had been held up only once, and it was during a trip he made to Haverhill, a city nearby. Luckily, he had few possesions with him besides the moderate amount of illegal substances he was planning on selling to the man who pulled a knife on him, so his losses were minimal. From that experience alone, he learned to stay in Ipswich and was making a steady income. All expenses considered, he figured he would be able to take another stab at New York City in six months if he was lucky. His plan required luck.

The sudden cracking of branches and rustling of leaves made him jump, but after a moment of confusion and certainty that he was being ambushed, [Censored], the kind manager of Movie Express, walked out from the woods and into the building.

"Hey, George," the man said. He was slightly overweight but had very animated features, always smiling big. He was friendly to everyone and knew all of his customers at the video rental store by name, along with their favorite genres. He was a good man, [Censored].

"Hey yourself." George had been waiting for him for almost a half hour. "You told me to be here at two." He could barely keep his eyes open.

"I know. I'm terribly sorry. I got caught up at home."

Yeah, you probably just smoked the last of what you bought the other day and lost track of time, George figured.

"You're lucky I like you." He pulled out the baggy containing the man's order and handed it over to him. "It's $100 tonight."

They concluded the transaction with a few practiced stealthy hand moves, and [Censored] left the building first. George didn't know why [Censored] insisted on being so stealthy with the exchange even while they were in the middle of the woods in an abandoned building at two in the morning, but he didn't question the culture that he was so new to. George always had the customers leave first. He didn't want to take the chance of being followed. He knew some of his customers, but others were complete strangers, phone numbers provided by Mike Cassidy, and he preffered they didn't know any details about his identity, if at all possible. It was easiest to keep the same practices with everyone he dealt with.

George sighed as he looked out the door to make sure his customer had gone and was beyond earshot. He didn't really care for his new profession, but he assumed it would allow him to get back to New York. He had to remind himself of that constantly. The stress was starting to wear him thin. He checked his watch. It was two thirty-four a.m. George stepped into the black of the night.

Gavin and Tanner

The marble countertops glistened in the light of the compact flourescants Gavin had just finished installing in the kitchen of his northside home. As it was the weekend, he was being productive with the time he had off from work. Not once had he sat with a newspaper or turned on the television. He told himself that if he was planning on the winning the affections of Laura Augustine, he had to become a man worthy of winning.

Earlier that day, he had cleaned the entire house from crown molding to original floors. He spent hours finding chores that needed to be tended to, most recently the caulking and repainting of the window trim and baseboards of the first floor. Not only had he completed that, but he had tended to the untouched cobwebs in the corners of the parlor ceilings, the dust caked books in the library, and even his son's room, against his trepidations.

He was apprehensive at first. There are a lot of things a parent can discover in an eighteen-year-old male's room that will shatter the illusion of their continuing childhood innocence – the kind that still holds to the parent's heart like a stubborn tick. Still, Gavin felt the need to be complete, and the house would not be clean unless every room was tended to. With caution, he entered the room and began tidying things up. At first, he found nothing out of the ordinary. After organizing the books on his son's desk, he moved on to folding clothes. After finding a shirt that needed to be hung, he opened the closet door.

When he found the paintings, he didn't know what to think. A year before when he was spending his time in his chair reading the newspaper and quite closed off to the world, he might have been cross. Unhappy, perhaps, that his son was bringing something unfamiliar and emotionally vulnerable into their efficient and rather emotionless household. Presently, he was more curious than anything, not to mention slightly disappointed that his son was hiding something from him. His thought process was disjointed and confused, but not cross. He looked at the one closest to the door. It was half finished, but the great skill his son had for the art was evident. Gavin wondered, When did he have the time to paint these? Surely he couldn't be doing both homework and producing the amount of canvases that were stacked in his closet. Since when did he fancy himself an artist? Why do so many of them seem unhappy and dark? There sure are a lot of self portraits. His hair doesn't look like that! Wait... is that even him? Why didn't he tell me?

In the end, he decided to leave the room untouched and pretend he had never discovered the paintings. It would be much easier if he ignored it. He would approach Tanner about them in time, when he knew what to say, but he was in the process of working out his own issues first. He returned to home improvement, slightly unnerved but not deterred from his goals.

Warming weather allowed him to do yardwork and exercise, as was required by his devotion to his goal. The landscaping, therefore, was immaculate, and he was beginning to return to good health. Life was good for Gavin Prior, though he was still coming up short.

For the life of him, he could not figure a way to initiate a relationship with the object of his desire. It was frustrating to no end when he would bump into Laura downtown at Bean or at Angela's Diner and have nothing to say, no way to initiate a conversation, only to watch her walk past without a word. They knew each other casually enough to smile and nod at one another, and Gavin survived on those hopes alone. Before his wife and brother had died, they would run into each other at large social events during the summer. Gavin's brother Daniel knew Laura from high school, and as they lived close by, he invited her to barbeques and pool parties — while he he was still alive, of course. Gavin and Laura would talk casually at the events and generally had good conversations, but Gavin was married and had no interest or temptation to be unfaithful at that time. He was, as he believed, blinded to Laura's beauty by his own values. It had been years since they had a proper conversation, and he wanted more than anything to change that.

As he was cleaning and improving the already modernized kitchen, he was plotting ways to have their stories cross paths, to force conversation and open her eyes to the truth that they were soulmates.

While he was beginning to polish the fixtures in the sink, the front door creaked open. Damn! I forgot to oil the hinges. How will Laura ever want to love a man who can't remember a simple task? Tanner walked into the house, though not into the kitchen where he usually fixed himself a meal-sized snack after school. The boy had the metabolism of a tiger.

"Tanner!" he called into the parlor.

"Yeah?"

"Come here." He would be impressed with the improvements to the kitchen, no doubt, and want to congratulate his father on a job well done.

"I'm busy!" he said, although he didn't sound it.

"Just come here!" Gavin heard his son rustling with his things and putting his backpack back on. A few moments later, he walked into the kitchen. The area surrounding his eye was black and blue and swollen. Gavin's chipper mood fell faster than metal scraps off their magnetic crane.

"What the hell happened to you?" He was stunned.

"It wasn't a fight, Dad, don't worry. I just got hit with a soccer ball." Tanner looked away, trying to avoid this kind of attention to his face.

"You're teammates have better aim than that. Whose girlfriend did you steal?" Gavin almost seemed perturbed with Tanner for letting himself get hit.

"We were playing a game against the new kid." He was sheepish, and his tone implied that he was embarassed about the situation.

"The whole team?" Gavin interrupted, incredulous.

"Er... yeah." His father wasn't buying it, so he tried to explain. "He came up with the idea. It was like he was a professional soccer player. Better than professional, Dad. It was unreal." Tanner paused and gently touched his eye, wincing at the sharp pain, "Anyway, we sort of taunted him and thought he was cheating, and then, well..." He pointed to his eye, needing no further explanation.

"Jesus, Tanner. The entire team against the new kid? You boys are more brutal than I thought. Maybe you deserved it after all." Gavin was blunt with his son, but his tone showed that he did care. Tanner didn't dare tell his father that the team lost the game. That would just make it worse. He knew his father wasn't trying to sound insensitive, but he couldn't help but be somewhat upset by the lack of support. He felt as if he had no one to talk to, no release besides his paintings. And no matter how much emotion he poured into them, they would never talk back, never tell him it would be okay. Some lessons were hard to learn but impossible to avoid. Tanner's anger had thawed, and he was presently just disappointed with himself. Realizing he handled the situation incorrectly, from Perran to Timothy, he gathered his things and grabbed a Coke from the fridge.

"I'm going to go do my homework," he said, ascending the steps.

"Okay, pal. G'night." Gavin knew no homework would be

done, but he didn't bring up the paintings. His son had enough for one day.

Laura and Mary

Mary rubbed her eyes, hoping to escape the fatigue that plagued her. She was in the seventh hour of an eight-hour shift at Movie Express and was tortured by the sight of the beautiful spring day just on the other side of the plate glass windows. While the ceiling inside was boring and grey and the flourscent light harsh, the sky outside was blue, and the sun was shining happily down on the grass that was beginning to return to its healthy Crayola green hue. It was a slow day for movie rentals, and she could see why.

Working at Movie Express was a rather brainless task, but it allowed her to catch up on her reading, despite reading less than normal in recent months. Her main responsibilities involved cataloging and entering new DVDs as they arrived from the distributors, scanning them and placing their cover art in the durable rental cases, applying barcodes, and entering their information into the computer database that kept track of rentals. She would then make space for them on the shelves by going into the catalog and finding which new releases were now old releases and moving them to the proper section in the right alphabetical order. Following this, she could then finally put the new arrivals on the shelves for customers to see and apply the yellow tape to the shelving where they were located to indicate a brand new release. Returns and late fees were similarly systematic in nature, and as no new movies had been released that day and the weather was nice enough to keep people outdoors, she sat idly behind the counter and read her latest fantasy of choice.

Considering her lack of customers and overall quiet nature of the day, imagine Mary's surprise when two uniformed police officers entered the store and approached the counter. She knew there was no possibility that she had done anything wrong, but police officers can cause a panic for just about anyone.

"Good afternoon, ma'am." They reminded her of the thieves in the original Home Alone movie.

"Hi, officers." Mary didn't know why police warranted special titles. If a firefighter had entered, she would not have said, "Hello, fireman."

"Ma'am, is Elijah Hart available at the moment?" Elijah was Mary's supervisor, the manager of Movie Express.

"Elijah didn't come to work today – at least not yet. He sleeps through his alarm sometimes. Is there a problem, officers?" It sounded so silly calling them that, but she was nervous and felt the need to be overly polite and respectful. She was suddenly aware of all her movements. Oh my God, I'm sweating so much. They'll notice that. But I haven't done anything wrong. It doesn't matter. If I sweat too much, they'll bring me in for questioning. Stop sweating! Breathe, Mary.

"That's okay. We'll stop in another time." The shorter officer tipped his hat, and the two walked out as quickly as they had come in. It was all over. As soon as her nerves had subsided, she began to wonder happened to Elijah that warranted the police looking for him at work. Normally, Elijah was always running a few minutes behind schedule, sometimes coming in an hour late after being "caught up at home" or "forgetting something." She had thought that it was completely acceptable that he had not shown up for work, but now she was worried.

Elijah was always so nice to Mary. Even before she had started to mature and learn the basics of socializing with others, he was kind to her, always answering her questions with a smile and asking her about her day, treating her hesitantly awkward answers as completely normal. He was a good man, that Elijah Hart.

For the rest of her shift, she was unnerved, mentally playing over various scenarios of what could have happened to her manager. Naturally, murder was one of the options she considered, but she couldn't think of a good reason anyone would want to harm Elijah. Perhaps there was a car accident on his way to work, but the roads were too quiet for a car accident – or at least she hoped they were. She was running through the brutal and gruesome possibilities in her head when Kelly, her replacement for the day, entered the store, a bell attached to the door alerting Mary of her arrival.

"Hey Mar! Slow today? It's freakin' gorgeous out." Kelly would probably always work at Movie Express.

"Yeah, yeah." Mary brushed her comments off. "Kelly, have you heard from Elijah? Two cops came in looking for him." Her worry made her awkwardness melt away. She wasn't yet completely confident, though moreso than usual.

"I talked to him this morning to find out what hours I was workin'. He seemed fine to me. Maybe he's back on his taxes or something." She shrugged and walked behind the counter to take over, logging into the computer-turned-cash register.

Mary finally exhaled. Of course! It had to be something simple, she was silly for letting her worries get so out of hand. She wasn't completely convinced, but she felt better about the situation and thanked Kelly for being on time to take over as she exited the store and walked out into the Tannery parking lot.

It was a short walk home, and Mary regretted not being able to walk around town and stay outside more; however, she had an important test looming over her head, and her GPA and impending graduation insisted she study. The lawn outside her small southside house was beginning to get overgrown with weeds. They were going to have to start doing yard work again, for spring was upon them.

When she pushed open the front door to her house, she heard her mother yelling at someone on the telephone. Surprisingly, however, she seemed sober.

"What letter?! I'm telling you, I didn't send a goddamned letter!" She paused, listening to the response that Mary couldn't hear. She considered going into the kitchen to attempt to eavesdrop but decided against it due to the probable confrontation it would cause.

"Ten years, and not a fucking peep! And now you simply waltz back to the east coast and start accusing me of things I didn't do?! Haven't you had enough, Joseph? Haven't you caused me enough grief? Or do you need to come back for more? Do you feed off it, get some sick pleasure from upsetting me?!" Her mother's voice cracked.

Obviously, it was her father on the phone. How appropriate that they would be having a screaming match, just like the last few years they were together – the only years, in fact, that Mary could remember. She didn't have any idea what they could be talking about. Mary hadn't received a letter from her father in months after losing the most recent one he sent, and to her knowledge, her mother hadn't talked to him either. Annoyed, Mary ascended the steps and went to her room to study.

Removing her books from her backpack, Mary wondered why her father would ever want to talk her mother again. They weren't on good terms. In fact, they were on some of the worst terms possible, saying unforgivable things to each other during their disintegration before Joseph packed his things and left. Also, what was this talk of a letter? She tried to put it out of her mind.

She heard muffled yells from below as her mother continued the argument, followed by the eventual slam of the phone on its receiver. It was distracting when she was trying to conjugate the imperfect form of fifty Spanish verbs she didn't know. As she looked over to her book for help with a definition, her bedroom door peeled open and hit the opposite wall with a loud bang.

"Why the hell would you do that, Mary?" her mother yelled at her, waving her hands in the air. Her hair was a frizzy mess.

"Do what?" She had no idea what she was getting yelled at for and furrowed her brow in confusion.

"You know exactly what. Your faaather says he got a letter from me inviting him to stay for a weekend this summer. He said it was so nicely written that he had already taken off work for the weekend." She lifted a finger at her daughter, accusing, "You know I'm crap with words, and I happen to know that you are obsessed with writing. What else am I supposed to think?" The words were so saturated with venom that they stung.

"Mom, I honestly have no idea what you're talking about. I didn't send him a letter." She put her hands up in defense as if about to receive a blow, despite both of them knowing it would never come to blows. Still, she was stunned at how much anger had built up in her mother, and she wondered why she was on the receiving end of it.

"Listen, Mary Anne Augustine. I did not send him a letter, and there is no one else who could have. I don't know why you did it, but I'm pissed off. Now I have to sit through two days of listening to your father bitch about the broads he chases and suffer his annoying attitude. You're going to regret sending it as soon as you see what a lowlife he is."

Mary paused, confused. "Wait... you're actually letting him come?"

Her mother rolled her eyes and batted her lashes. Her anger melted away as she tried to look casual but only succeeded in looking guilty. "Well, he already requested time off..." She was weak.

PART THREE

Tanner

Ten minutes left of class...

Nine minutes fifty-seven seconds...

Nine minutes fifty-five seconds, twenty-three miliseconds...

Nine minutes fifty-three seconds, forty-two miliseconds, four nanoseconds...

So went the thoughts of Tanner and every other senior in Ms. Ramsay's advanced English class that Friday. Summer was beginning to break through the mild spring weather, and classes were ending in a few short weeks. Every day was a struggle just to survive until the last bell at two fifteen when they would all be free to enjoy the freedom and weather and adult independence that they deserved. They were grown men and women! Going to college! Invincible!

Like a heroin addict gripping the Earth to stop it from spinning during detox or a track star about to launch from the starting line into a sprint toward Olympic gold, Tanner Prior gripped his desk as he watched the clock high on the wall. He was counting down the minutes toward what was predicted to be a weather perfect and responsibility free weekend. The handsome outcast (an idiot, despite his soccer skills that were so vehemently explained as cheating) was debating the early life of Shakespeare with the eccentric instructor, much to the dismay of Tanner and his peers, who were rooting for a lull in conversation that would result in early dismissal.

"Ah, but isn't it poetic and fitting that he should die on his day of birth?" Ms. Ramsay questioned, raising her eyebrows at the boy.

"Tabe—er, uh, Madaam Ramsay, it may be poetic, but it is utterly unbelievable. He was not born on April 23, but rather on April 21. Trust me." He said the last words with such authority.

What a prick, thought Tanner and several others in the class.

Nina, one of foreign students, raised her hand. "Why does it matter when he was born?" she asked, addressing both of them. They both thought such a question perposterous and let her know it. It quickly dissolved from a class discussion to a private argument among the three. The rest of the class was given the implied privilege to talk amongst themselves.

Timothy had been absent for two days now, and Tanner had not heard from him. They had gotten into a silly argument about the amount of time they spent together and were not on speaking terms. Still, Tanner worried about his best friend, his confidant.

The argument had started like any of their other squabbles. Tanner had called Timothy to join him downtown the weekend prior, and upon Timothy's invitation to stay the night at his place, had grown defensive and called Timothy "clingy." This, of course went down like sour milk, and Timothy's frustration with Tanner's mood swings erupted, both of them yelling at each other and calling out names that would make their parents cringe.

"Hey, have you heard why Timothy hasn't been in school?" Tanner leaned in and asked Ricky, who was aware of their recent squabbles.

"No, but I'll text him." He pulled out his phone and tapped away, slipping it back into his pocket when he was done.

"Thanks," Tanner said, slightly embarrassed.

"No problem." Ricky hesitated, not sure if he should continue. "Why are you guys fighting anyway? You are best friends."

"Long story." He wasn't sure why he got so frustrated and confused all the time, let alone why they fought about it. Thankfully, Ricky let the issue go, and the two started to discuss their latest soccer practice before they were interrupted by two quiet buzzes coming from below the table.

"Must be Timothy," Ricky said, pulling out his phone again. "Let's see. He says he's sick today and... what the hell?" He suddenly looked angry.

"What?"

"He's quit the team! We only have a week left, and the little shit is quitting the team!" Ricky was incredulous. Timothy was one of their best forwards.

Tanner didn't say anything at first. He just looked back at Ricky confused, one eyebrow raised. His brain was firing on all cylindars trying to understand Timothy's reasoning. His first thoughts wandered to their disagreement, but he hesitantly dismissed it as it was too small an argument to make such a unreasonable decision. He paused, still silent. No other reasons filled the void. As well as he knew Timothy, he was still coming up blank. *Why the fuck did he quit?*

The remaining minutes of class passed slower than proposed legislation. Tanner couldn't keep himself distracted, despite many attempts. He considered a new composition for a painting he was planning on starting, going for a walk on the boardwalk, and his plans for the summer, but they all came back to Timothy and his absence. It was unquestionably frustrating.

When finally the bell did ring, Tanner walked briskly out the door and onto the finally green and healthy lawn outside the building. Unlocking his cellphone with a stroke of his finger, he speed dialed Timothy. It rang one time more than usual before he picked up.

"What?" He sounded cranky.

"Timothy, what is this I hear about you quitting the team?" Tanner tried his best to sound concerned. He knew that although they were technically fighting, if Timothy really did quit the team, something must have happened.

"Yeah what about it?" He WAS cranky.

"Well, is everything okay?"

"WHY THE HELL WOULD YOU CARE!?" *Click.*

Tanner stood there with his phone to his ear, stunned. *This couldn't be because of the argument. Timothy must have heard a rumor of some sort about him or something he said. God, had he said anything bad about the guy recently?* He didn't think so. He was pretty sure he never had anything but good things to say about him, unless they were arguing, of course. In that case, he would just bad mouth him to his face and keep quiet around everyone else anyway.

It ended up being quite the perfect day, weather wise at least. The sun shone down on the newly green grass, the cloudless blue sky providing perfect constrast to the red of the brick buildings. Suddenly, Tanner wanted nothing more than for Timothy to be happy again and to share the first summer day together with him like every year before. Knowing that he just needed to clear his head, he decided to go for a walk.

The people of Ipswich came out of hibernation en masse, like earthworms after a storm. As Tanner walked through town, he spotted activity outside the majority of the restored homes. Grandfathers playing catch with their barely-able-to-walk grandchildren, husbands tending to the landscaping that was growing faster than Audrey II in Little Shop of Horrors, and the warm weather enticing everyone outdoors.

After a half hour, he found himself at the entrance to Maudson State Park. The groundskeepers no longer patrolled daily, leaving the large administrative building abandoned and overgrown, even though it was still used on occasion. As such, the recent weather caused the fields at the entrance to be slightly in need of a mowing, and Tanner did not spot a single other soul present. He was never deterred by the possibility of ticks, so he stepped over the old stone wall and into the park. He imagined that connecting with nature would soothe his nerves or tickle his muse for another painting.

Crossing the field, the breeze died down, and the sun warmed the back of his neck. Eventually, he even started to get hot, though not uncomfortably so. It would be another few minutes before he reached the comfort of the shady woods, so he unbuttoned his oxford shirt to let what little wind his forward movement created pass through more easily.

Tanner loved Maudson and usually revered any time he got spend there, feeling like a lone pioneer in the days before technology, sports, arguments with your best friend, confusion, and frustration. When he was alone surrounded by the trees, accompanied only by birds and deer, all those things just melted away. Today, however, his lonliness stayed firmly rooted in his conciousness.

He entered the forest on a mulched pathway, the sunlight dancing through the branches and painting patterns on the Nemerov floor. After some time, he turned a corner on the path and came to an old stone bridge that passed in an arch over a large creek. As he approached, he saw a beautiful doe grazing the grass on the opposite side. He immediately slowed his walk to observe but did not stop. Another doe emerged from the trees and joined the first, grazing next to it. With a crunch, Tanner accidentally broke a fallen branch on the path. The startled deer looked up in surprise and bounded back into the safety of the trees from which they came.

"You should really watch where you step."

Tanner flinched so hard his muscles threatened to cramp. The voice had come from the trees above, and he quickly and defensively looked around to see who it was. At once, he spotted the source. Perran Nemerov was sitting on a branch twenty feet off the ground, wearing only brown linen pants, silently taking bites out of a pear.

"Jesus Christ! What are you doing up there? Were you spying on me?" Tanner's heart was still beating quickly, and he was creeped out by the strange boy lounging and looking so comfortable up in the branches.

"I shouldn't have to remind you that you're the one who wandered in on me and those nice animals. Perhaps you should be more observant of your surroundings."

Tanner noticed that the strange boy had tattoos on his chest along his collarbone, almost forming a necklace of designs. They were a strange mix between tribal and floral and were similarly seen around his upper arms below the shoulder as well. They were dark – not colored or overly detailed – but the ink seemed inexplicably strange, days old at most.

Perran finished his pear, raised his eyebrows once with his final chews, and started swinging down to the forest floor, branch to branch like an Olympic gymnast. Finally, he was standing before Tanner. Even with his pefect posture, he fell a few inches shorter than the startled soccer player, who seemed to have regained his composure.

Tanner felt like he should make conversation but didn't know what to say. It was an awkward situation.

"So... er... what are you doing here?" He shrugged his

shoulders. He was too tired to be defensive or tell the boy to bug off, so he resigned himself to forced civil conversation.

"I'm enjoying the weather, enjoying my roots, spending some time with those deer you scared away." He motioned to the clearing in which the deer had been moments before. "I imagine by and large you came here to do the same thing?" They started walking down the path. Tanner noted that Perran spoke more like an adult than the students his age.

"Yeah, you just gotta escape sometimes, you know?" His discomfort was palpable. Perran considered what he said for a moment, though in Tanner's eyes it was hardly a comment worth thinking about. Finally, Perran spoke.

"You should ask yourself if you're in the right situation if you ever feel like you have to escape, don't you think?" Perran's face was unnervingly calm. He seemed to be genuinely curious about Tanner's off handed statement. Tanner felt like he was suddenly a guest in his house, allowing an awkward silence. He changed the subject.

"So, uh... when did you get those tattoos?" he asked, gesturing toward the designs. Perran looked down and made a face that suggested he forgot he even had them.

"Oh these?" His gaze returned to Tanner. "I've had those for as long as I can remember." He shrugged his shoulders.

"That long, eh?" Tanner didn't know why they were talking. He didn't know why he couldn't just have left the boy alone and not scared the deer away. He just wanted to escape his thoughts.

"Why are you here, Tanner Prior?" Perran stopped walking. They had come to a small clearing that allowed the sun to break through the canopy. The smell of pine was strong. Tanner stared back at the boy, knowing that he had never really given him a chance. From what he could tell, although extremely unusual, Perran seemed to be wise beyond his years and willing to connect and be friends. He was talented and had shown that he could hold his own but always seemed to extend a hand to those who needed it. The frustration and loneliness were present, and here was someone who was smart and willing to listen, holding the door open for him to release the negativity. He only had to step through. Finally, someone was willing to listen – someone who, as far as Tanner could tell, wouldn't gossip or spread his story. Making his most mature decision in recent months, Tanner finally decided to give the guy a shot.

"It's hard to explain," he started, unsure if he should continue. "Timothy and me have been disagreeing a lot lately. I don't know if you know this, but we are... well, we're pretty much best buds since kindergarten. I just... I don't know. I don't understand why he says certain things he says. It's not that he's ever mean to me. I just get frustrated when I don't know what's going on with me and him, and I guess if I feel vulnerable, I just... snap."

Perran nodded and stepped over to a tree stump, sitting down and putting his elbows on his knees with his hands interlocked.

"It's been happening more and more lately." It was all flowing at this point, like water bursting over the dam. "I feel like I'm losing my best friend. It doesn't help that my dad has been acting so different lately, which makes me feel like everything is getting turned upside down, and I guess I just feel..." Tanner paused. He had never felt so vulnerable, especially with someone he knew so little. He decided that he had already gone this far and continued, "I guess I just feel alone."

The two were silent for a moment. Perran looked up at Tanner, who stood and sighed. Perran stood as well and looked over to him.

"And what would you want to happen now, if you could have any outcome you wanted? What would be ideal?"

Tanner thought about it for a moment. He thought about Timothy coming back into his life, seeing his caring green eyes and cheerful smile again. He had these thoughts but said simply, "I don't know."

"Do you truly not know, or are you just afraid to admit what has become apparent?"

"What are you talking about?" Tanner said, slightly defensive, retreating to the forced confusion that allowed him to not even address the issues he knew to be true with his own mind.

In that moment, Perran swept in and pecked Tanner on the lips, though not aggresively or seemingly for his own wants, his eyes never losing their tone of concentration and serenity. Tanner's varsity sports upbringing instinctively told him to swing, though truly, he was too stunned to have any control over his actions, and it was halfhearted at best. As he did, Perran leaped backwards and swung himself with one arm around the trunk of the tree from which he came. With a graceful momentum, he propelled himself up onto one of the branches and began ascending back into the safety of the tree. Before Tanner could shout or yell at the invasion, Perran looked down at him with a caring, yet strangely parental look upon his face.

"It would seem it is time you stop trying to understand others, Tanner Prior, and start trying to understand yourself." He smiled and started climbing limb by limb higher and higher into the trees, carelessly enjoying the warm spring day.

Tanner stood dazed below. He could still feel the violation upon his face. But was it even that? Was he even made? He looked up into the trees where the boy had been but only saw swaying branches and heard only the rustling of leaves. Perran was gone. The sun and nature were indifferent and did not change with his mood like the movies suggested they may. Still, it was a beautiful day, but it no longer was such a treat. He couldn't decide whether he was angry and mad or lonely and regretful. Though he had swung in reflex, the contact of another person so gently comforted him, as much as he hated to admit it. Eyes unfocused, he walked slowly out of the woods and across the field, heading back toward town, looking neither at the ground nor the scenery around him. He was lost entirely in the depths of his own thoughts.

Mary

Sleeping with the windows open in Ipswich was a summertime treat. Rare was the weather the perfect mix of mid-seventies and low humidity that allowed a gentle breeze to brush against your face as your drifted off to sleep. Lucky enough was Mary to be able to enjoy such a night during her last school week in May. Seniors at Ipswich High were released from the obligation of classes several weeks before their underclassmen counterparts, so the mid-May warmth was enough to keep her comfortable. It was the type of weather that allowed one to wake completely rested at nine in the morning, unable to sleep another wink.

A very loud knocking at the door was almost worse than a school-year alarm clock. Jarred awake by the sudden pounding, Mary groggily opened her eyes and looked over to the door.

"I'm awake, I'm awake!" she yelled at the closed door, knowing her mother was on the other side, tapping her foot impatiently like she always did. She kicked her blankets off, her knee cracking as she pushed them off the edge of the bed and stretched her arms high over her head with a yawn. She looked over to her desk that was unusually clear of its normal mess of papers and printed fan fiction. Recently, she had been exploring mysteries as opposed to fantasy. It was something she had never tried before, but she had to admit she was thoroughly enjoying all the new aspects and plots that she hadn't yet experienced.

Her room smelled of fresh-cut grass and the subtle undertones of lilac that drifted in from the neighbor's overgrowth of flowers. She looked out on to the street that was completely abandoned. From out of the corner of her eye, she thought she saw someone turn the corner, but when she looked, there was nothing there.

She walked downstairs to the kitchen, where she grabbed an apple from the refrigerator before grabbing her purse and heading out the front door. As she walked out on to the porch. she noticed a bouquet of vibrant fresh flowers sitting on the dirty welcome mat, providing a gentle visual irony. Mary smiled in spite of herself and bent down and picked up the bouquet, inspecting it for a card or note of some sort. It was not wrapped in plastic or anything commercial looking, but just a simple piece of twine. At one of the ends of string, she saw a single piece of paper upon which was written in perfect cursive "For Laura."

It was surprising, to say the least, that her mother was receiving flowers, but then Mary realized that her father was coming back into town. It was very out of character, or so she assumed, but then again, she didn't really know her father at all. She had the strange sense that it might be some sort of manipulation. Shrugging it off (as she didn't really care either way about her father), she brought the flowers inside and placed them on the kitchen counter before heading back outside and locking the front door behind her.

Between the time she had woken up and the time she exited her house, it had warmed considerably. Still, it was not uncomfortably hot for a summer day, and Mary walked slowly through her southside neighborhood and toward town. Strolling along looking at her various neighbors' attempts at gardening, her thoughts drifted to George. She knew that she was developing a bit of a crush on him and couldn't help but imagine how it would feel had the flowers on her doorstep been addressed to her. Still, if her developing social skills taught her anything, it was to take things one step at a time and relax.

Before she knew it, she was at the door of Angela's Diner. As she opened the door, the smell of frying bacon and freshly brewed coffee nearly overwhelmed her. There was little to compare with the smell of the undefensibly unhealthy diner food on a comfortable summer morning. She waited, as everyone does, slightly awkwardly at the front of the restaurant to spot an available seat at a small table. Mary always felt guilty sitting at large tables when she was all by herself. Both George and her Spanish instructor, Ms. Girard, were working as servers, clearing tables and taking orders, refilling coffees, and balancing plates on their forearms.

Instead of buddying up to George immediately and seeming too eager for her own good, Mary decided to try olaying the hard-to-get card. She read about it in one of her recent mysteries, and it apparently worked like a charm with men. Therefore, instead of approaching George like she usually would for a table, she walked up to her Ms. Girard and said hello.

"Good morning, Ms. Girard. Think I could grab a seat?" she smiled.

"Hola, chica." Barry Ann Girard was Irish American but had a passion for the Spanish language, "Si, si. Take a seat wherever te gusta." The perfect Spanish accent seem somehow wrong coming out of such a freckled face.

"Thanks." Mary sat down at a small two-topper that was clearly not part of George's territory for the day. "How have you been? Are you excited to have the summer off?"

"I've been pretty great," Barry Ann smiled, throwing her rag over her shoulder and leaning on the counter next to her. "But you must be even more excited for summer than I am! Do you know where you are going to college yet?"

Awkward. As of yet, Mary still hadn't been planning on going to college. Despite all of her advances, she still held tight to the dream of becoming an overnight success as an author. There were several schools in the area still offering rolling admissions, though she still was wary.

"No news on the college front yet. I might end up taking some time off," Mary replied, tactfully she thought. Barry Ann grinned in response, though it was clear she was not a fan of the increasingly popular "time off after graduation" option. The two ladies exchanged pleasantries as Barry Ann excused herself to tend to some other tables, and Mary was left alone, compulsively fiddling with her fork.

She could feel George looking at her as Barry Ann brought her over her apple juice and small bowl of grits and brown sugar. She hoped that her choice to be served by her teacher as opposed to George didn't make him mad or upset. She only wanted to make him jealous. She was new to all this and was understandably nervous about the mindgames involved in young adult romance. She didn't question that he liked her, even though the only evidence she had were their meaningful conversations.

As she slowly ate her grits, she looked around at the other customers that chose to have their breakfast at the diner that morning. In the far corner was Elijah Hart, who had returned to Movie Express after an unexplained week of absence. Wherever he had been or whatever had happened no one knew, but he had lost a bit of his charm and appeal since his return. His glances up from his food were generally directed at George, looking worried or uneasy about something or other. Mary disregarded it. At the large table near the window sat a couple of the private school boys. She knew them to be soccer players but didn't know any of them personally. They weren't talking much. Along the bar stools overlooking the griddles sat the older generation of Ipswich. The townies that never left, they would come to Angela's Diner religiously day in and day out, rain or shine, as the surroundings were familiar and comfortable and the servers were like family to them.

A bell somewhere near the door jingled as the handsome boy she knew to be Tanner Prior, one of the private school soccer stars, walked into the diner. She noticed that the sky had turned grey, threatening rain at any moment, and she suddenly remembered that she had forgotten an umbrella). Moments later, she heard the loud peel of a chair being pushed back a bit too quickly, and one of the soccer players at the other table walked out, forcefully knocking shoulders with Tanner as he stormed past and out the door into the pre-rain mist. Mary rolled her eyes. Saint Andrews drama was more than she could handle. As she finished up the last of her food and was getting her money out, George approached.

"Hey, Mary. How are you?" he asked, nonchalant.

"Hey, George. I'd love to chat, but I actually have to get home. I'll see you later." She was better at the game than she thought. George looked somewhat surprised, but not as upset as she had wanted him to be.

"See ya, then" He said the last word almost like a question, so unused to being blown off so quickly by her.

In truth, she didn't have to get home. Positive that she was mastering the hard-to-get routine, she threw down enough money for her food and a generous tip on her table. She smirked as she threw her purse over her shoulder and walked out of the diner, unable to withhold a grin for how well she was doing playing the new game of romance.

Joseph, Laura, and Mary

Route 95 was a familiar sight. No matter where someone from the area ended up in life, if they grew up along coastal New England, they instantly knew they were in familiar territory when they were greeted by the eight-lane highway. It was lined with identical trees, similar overpasses and exits in almost all cases, and the speed limit an average fifteen miles per hour over the posted sixty-five maximum.

There was fairly light traffic as the old white pickup truck hurtled down the highway through the summertime rain shower, heading toward northern Massachusetts with a grey sky above. Joseph Augustine was drumming on the steering wheel as Metallica (a recent discovery of his) blared through the tin sounding stock speakers. Joseph was a gangly man, thin but appearing unhealthy, with bags under his small eyes and a mess of blonde hair slowly blending to grey. He was nearly finished with the four-and-half-hour trip up from New York City, where he presently was working at the Q-Mart near Penn Station. He had come to the city after a failed attempt at transforming himself into a successful agent for budding actresses in Los Angeles. Joseph had made somewhat of a career out of others' dashed hopes, inviting young women who didn't quite have the looks for cameras to places like Massachsetts, where they could still be stars. His multiple McJobs such as his gig at Q-Mart just supplemented to his income, or so he told himself. Eventually, he tired of the rejection and was having more and more trouble pawning off his story. Who didn't claim they had connections in LA? Everyone was suspicious, especially since he lacked the common sense to even print an exaggerative business card.

Selma Rodriguez was the name of the woman that had secured his fate as a failure in Los Angeles. She was short, but bubbly and exotic, beautiful and sexy, a firecracker of a woman. Joseph was instantly drawn to her and approached her at a bar downtown called Rush. He played his normal routine of the agent looking for talent for a particular part he knew of through a friend. She ate it up, or so it seemed. When he got her back to his apartment that night, she wanted to try some more exciting things in the bedroom, and Joseph happily obliged, having had a lull in prurient activity for some time. It was only after she had stolen his wallet, iPod, and laptop while he was tied to the bedposts with faux silk scarves that he realized he had made a mistake. He legitimately thought she was playing a prank on him at first, but after a half hour of waiting alone tied to his bed, he began to panic, not to mention to feel like a fool. Three days and many embarassing phone calls to the bank and police station later, he packed his things into his pickup and decided to give New York a try.

He had only been living in New York for a couple of months when the letter from Laura arrived. There wasn't much information in it. It simply read:

> J,
> Both myself and your daughter would like to see you. She is blossoming into a woman, and it pains me to be the only parent to see her grow. I miss you more than words can describe.
> Still yours,
> L

As he had yet to establish himself in New York and the loneliness was beginning to show its ugly head, he had taken off work for a weekend and decided to visit the family he had left behind. He had never imagined going back, but with things as low as they were for him, it seemed a fitting concession to make for the comfort (and possible action) it would give him. When he called to let his ex-wife know that he would be visiting, she denied having sent the letter in the first place. He knew better than to believe her, though, deciding that she was probably just embarassed about the whole thing – particularly that "I miss you more than words can describe" part.

Finally approaching Exit 56, Joseph clicked on his turn

signal and veered to the right, exiting the homogeneous highway and turning on to the rural street that led to Ipswich. After passing the farms and wetlands that lined the street, the Ipswich windmill (a recent addition to the landscape) came into view, and the buildings started appearing closer together. Like a time machine, his car went from passing an industrial park, to entering the southside of town with its mid-century developments, to High Street lined with houses dating back to the Revolution. It was all lost on him, though, because he couldn't care much less about architecture. What he found much more enthralling was another swig of the vodka and Coke was stealthily disguised in his coffee traveler in the front seat cup holder.

The route was familiar and automatic, which Joseph thought strange. After ten years and a life quite different from the one he had known here, his hands still naturally turned the right directions and thoughtlessly took him on the quickest route to his old home. He arrived in front of the small suburban house and stepped out of the car into the rain, his nerves escalating with each step closer to the front door.

Mary seriously regretted not bringing an umbrella to the diner with her. On her walk home, it had started to rain. It wasn't a drenching downpour, but enough to make her uncomfortable. She tried her hardest to let go of her instinct to shirk the idea of wet clothes and simply enjoy the fact that it was warm enough to rain without freezing. She was pleased with herself for how nonchalant she had acted in front of George, imagining him back at the diner pining over her and wishing for her return. She smiled to herself.

As she was revelling in her newfound social skills and clever conversational manuevers, her phone rang from her pocket. Deciding that it wasn't raining hard enough to ignore the call, she answered.

"Hello?" People always answered calls like they were unsure if someone was actually on the other line, despite statistics to the contrary.

"Hey, Mary, it's George." Jackpot.

"Hey, George." She stayed calm. "What's up?"

"Well, since we didn't get to talk much today, I was wondering if you wanted to hang out and do something later this week." He was casual, but Mary knew she had him. She tried to play it cool and told herself that she couldn't automatically agree and seem too eager. She couldn't expose that she was playing the game.

"Well, this week is busy, but what are you doing on the 29th? I'm free then. Maybe you could come over and watch a movie or something." Mary had heard that watching a movie was code for a date. She wasn't sure about this but knew that a movie was a safe bet with George.

"Sure, that sounds great. Hey, I gotta get back to work, though, so I'll talk to you later." She could hear in the background that this was probably true.

"Bye, George." She smiled to herself. She still had her game.

The smile quickly changed into an expression of confusion as she rounded the corner to her street and saw a white pickup truck in her driveway. She ran through a mental checklist of all the neighbors' cars and came up blank. No one she knew had a white pickup. And then it came to her. Dad's here. Her good mood faltered, flickered, gave the impression it may stick around, and then vanished faster than Professor Quirrel at the end of Harry Potter and the Sorcerer's Stone. She was suddenly extremely apprehensive and decided she would just say hello and then quickly disappear to her room to work on her latest writing endeavor.

Doors make entirely too much noise, Mary noted as she opened the front door with a loud squeak. Her mother and father came to the entryway from the kitchen. Mary hardly recognized her father. Of course, he had become a bit of a blur to her, so seeing him manifested in the flesh standing there next to her mother was an odd experience, not unlike seeing a celebrity in person for the first time only to discover they look nothing like their television self. Being caught in the rain worked to Mary's advantage, as when her mother and father approached for hugs, they quickly pulled their arms back and smiled as if she had pulled a clever prank on them.

"Ah, you were always smart, Mary. Too big for hugs now?" Her father chuckled as if what he said was even remotely funny. She cringed and made a face at him. Who is this man? What in God's name is he doing back here?

"I have a lot of homework to do," she said, knowing that her mother could see through her blatant lie.

"Oh. Well, study, study, study." He spoke quickly, like he was on speed, but slurred his Ss as if he were drunk. She wondered if he was drunk, thinking it would be strangely appropriate, through she didn't know exactly why. She vaguely remembered him being drunk when she was a child, though at the time, she wasn't quite sure what it meant to be drunk.

She retreated to her bedroom, letting her mother deal with the mess. The woman had made her bed, and now she had to sleep in it.

Laura was finding it difficult to be herself. She had played situation over in her head a million times, rehearsing the perfect things to say, the right body language, everything down to the placement of the flowers in the kitchen that would make Joseph realize what a mistake he had made in leaving and instill in him an unquenchable thirst to return. Currently, it appeared that he wasn't noticing any of it. Laura smelled the faint tang of alcohol in the room and assumed she must have spilled some the night before. As if reading her mind, Joseph broke the silence.

"So, shall we have a drink?" he asked, motioning his head to the liquor cabinet. Like a shrine of some sort, it had remained in the same place for ten years.

"What would you like?" She wasn't going to have anything alcoholic this time. She had resolved to stay sober. She had to.

"Scotch is fine."

Laura walked over to the cabinet and made her ex-husband his drink, which she knew he preferred on the rocks. For herself, she filled a tall glass with Diet Coke. He thought she was having rum as well, but she didn't bother to correct him. A week before, while she was on her way to work after a night of drowning her insecurities in a bath of gin and tonic, she had made the promise to herself. The sun was shining brightly that day, an enemy of her head that pounded in protest every time the light caused a sparkle or glare through her windshield. The smell of alcohol lingered on her breath, despite having brushed her teeth twice to get rid of it. It emanated from her pores. At the intersection of High and State Streets, she met a red light. Her reflection waited in the visor mirror, begging to be seen. Reluctantly and defeated, she pulled down the flap and greeted herself for the first time that morning. She wore little makeup, and her hair shone in the morning sun because she had showered only minutes before. It was her eyes that made her sad. Barely slits, with the right eye threatening to shut completely, she could hardly keep them open. Each ray of sunlight slammed into her skull with the force of a hammer, and her eyes were her last line of defense, trying to deflect the attack. The odor of alcohol was the smell of her body's battle. Her thoughts turned to Joseph's coming visit. She thought of his problems with drugs and alcohol and how badly it had hurt their family, how it had destroyed the life that she pined for. Am I any better? she asked herself.

"This has to stop," she told her dashboard, gripping the steering wheel firmly. She had not had a drink since, despite the temptation. It called to her from the cabinet and laughed at her from the windows of the grocery store, taunting her. Still, her resolve was strong, and she somehow connected her strength in resistance to the return of happiness to her family. If she could turn alcohol away, she thought her fortune would undoubtedly improve.

Laura looked over at Joseph.

"So?"

"So."

It was an awkward beginning. At first, neither of them knew what to talk about. Laura eventually brought up Vermont family vacation that was so fondly embedded in her memory. The scotch kept flowing, and before long, Joseph was leading the stories, though instead of talking of family stories like Laura would have preferred, he talked about his exploits in Los Angeles. They began innocently enough. At first there were descriptions of locations and businesses. Five drinks in, however, at the point of serving himself, Joseph started bringing up memorable trysts and exploits with girls he had met after he left his wife. Laura knew she had lost at this point and could feel the tears waiting behind her eyelids for a safe time to escape, but she held them back, holding on to hope that things could still turn around. Frantically, she needed a new fantasy. She needed a new way to imagine how this meeting would conclude. Perhaps he would talk about all these girls and suddenly say something along the lines of "They could never compare to you," and they would embrace and live happily ever after. She knew she was just playing the fool at this point, but she wouldn't admit it to herself. She couldn't.

He was starting to slur his words, leaning back on the couch like a slob. Laura's admiration for the man had melted away. He had been talking about some blond bimbo named Qristal (spelled, yes, with a Q) that he never got to bed. He was hardly making sense anymore. Laura realized in that instant what a fool she had been. The disappointment was almost too much to bear. Who was this man? This was not the man of her memories. This was a scummball who was tarnishing her home with his presence. She looked over at him and couldn't believe her eyes. He was rubbing himself through his pants as, eyes half open, he kept on with the stories about Q-tip or whatever her name was. Laura was just about to kindly excuse herself so she could escape to her room to let free some emotions when he said it – the straw that broke the camel's back. And the damage to the poor camel was nothing compared to how he forever shattered her fantasies of him.

"So, are we gonna bang or what?"

There was a pause as Laura struggled to confirm that she had heard him correctly, followed by a rumbling from beneath. The floor shook. The floorboards splintered into a thousand tiny daggers as the yellow flames erupted from beneath, licking the furniture and ceiling, lava boiling onto the floor of the room. Satan himself rose from beneath as all hell was let loose.

"WHO THE HELL DO YOU THINK YOU, ARE YOU LITTLE PIECE OF WASHED-UP SHIT? GET THE HELL OUT OF MY HOUSE, YOU BASTARD!" Laura's voice boomed as though she herself was God of the underworld. Joseph looked up stunned, as if he had just woken up. Mary ran to the banister to look down to make sure everything was alright. Somewhere, a dog was howling. The rain pounded down on the roof in a thousand tiny pats – the only noise Joseph could hear as he looked up in horror at the fiery hatred emanating from Laura's eyes.

"Well," Joseph said, scrunching up his face. "Well... fuck

you too." Realizing he was an unwanted guest, he spit on the ground and stormed out, the smell of alcohol hanging on the air. Laura was trembling violently as she walked into the kitchen and picked up the phone.

"Yes... um... I need a taxi at 34 South Atkinson Road." She could barely get the words out and muttered a choked up "Thank you" as she slowly put the phone back into its holder with unsteady hands. She collapsed onto the floor, crying.

Mary ran down the stairs and knelt down next to her mother, putting a comforting hand on her back, "It's okay, Mom." She cradled her mother as she mourned the loss of her fantasy – a daughter holding her mother, the timeless and inevitable reversal of roles. This was as close as they would get to being a family.

Gavin

Gavin sat in his favorite chair at Bean in downtown Ipswich, sipping his espresso and looking out on the grey sky that made the Merrimack River seem black and murky. Several sailboats were out in the river, having escaped their moorings to brave the choppy waves. Shortly, they would have to return, Gavin considered. It would get too choppy when the wind picked up and the rain started pouring at its full power.

As it were, Gavin was comforted by the crackling of the fireplace, (which owners Todd and Colleen kept burning year round for atmosphere) and the smell of incense burning somewhere by the counter. He nibbled on a raspberry scone and waffled in between observing the outdoors and other people in the shop and reading the novel he had brought along with him for the day. His thoughts drifted to Laura as they so often did. He had seen her several days before, and she hadn't looked her best, the redness obvious even from underneath the sunglasses she was wearing. Her movements had somehow been just a bit too calculated. She was obviously upset about something. He hoped she was okay.

His thoughts on those he cared about, he considered Tanner's recent change in behavior. Gavin and his son were never that close, with Gavin concerning himself mostly with inspiring Tanner to be the best he could be with his natural athletic talent. He knew that his son had a future ahead of him in soccer if he wanted it and if the right amount of effort and perseverance was applied. Lately, though, he had started to question whether he wanted it as much as he originally thought he did. Tanner had been very moody and still hadn't told Gavin about his paintings. Gavin still couldn't figure out why his son painted so much. His friends had stopped coming over, and the boy just locked himself up in his bedroom under the transparently false pretense of doing his homework. Please. Years ago, when Gavin was more of a recluse, that excuse may have passed, but ever since his awakening in the winter – that sudden sudden awareness of the world and community and possibility of relationships – he he knew better. He of course still hoped that his son would realize his potential and turn his mind back to his athletics, but more than that, he hoped Tanner was okay. If only there were only an easy way to connect without the inevitable awkwardness that would ensue from a historically distant and aloof man addressing his similarly reclusive son for an emotional conversation. Was it even possible for them to become close this late in the game?

Gavin looked out the window. Somewhere out in the river, a sailor rode his dinghy toward his ship that was moored several hundred feet into the channel. The choppy waves and strong current seemed to push him back every time he made any progress toward his vessel. Foamy water splashed over the sides and into the inflated boat as it struggled. Just as it appeared he would have to turn back, a rogue wave gave the small boat the final push it needed, and it surfed the swell toward its destination, the sailor throwing a rope onto the larger sailboat and ferociously tying the dinghy so he would not be lost again to the current. Gavin exhaled, having watched the entire episode with bated breath.

Realizing there was nothing left of his scone but crumbs and his espresso was long gone, Gavin closed his book and put it back in his briefcase that leaned against the side of his favorite wing-back chair. Rising, he looked around the rest of the cafe, which was surprisingly empty except for the odd shaggy haired boy who sat in the far corner, reading again what appeared to be an antique book. When Gavin walked past, the boy looked over the top of his book watching him intently. The kid always seemed to be in the background, and not knowing who he was, Gavin was always unnerved by his presence at Bean.

When he walked out of the cafe and on to the brick sidewalks of downtown Ipswich, he was fortunate enough to not be subject to the rain characteristic of recent weeks, though there was a slight mist washing over his face, playfully dancing on the wind. Normally, Gavin took the car downtown, despite living only a few streets away. It had become a habit one winter and unfortunately lasted long into the years ahead.

In recent months, though, he had gone back to walking the five minutes it took to go downtown and enjoyed the architecture and gardens of the homes around him. He was slowly integrating himself back into the community after years of living like a hermit.

The front door of the Prior household no longer squeaked when it was opened, for it had been one among many of the long neglected household tasks on Gavin's recent to-do list. The front yard was neatly manicured, the lights in the house were all replaced with money saving compact florescent bulbs, the living room had been painted a deep red, and the dining room ceiling was patched of the water damage that had lingered for ages. Indeed, their home on Green Street looked better than it had in a decade.

Gavin entered and immediately became nervous. He had been thinking about calling Laura for weeks and asking her out to dinner. Whenever he was around a phone, his nerves acted up, but today was different. He knew he had to do it. Worrying and waiting will accomplish nothing, he concluded. He approached the phone, and the lights seemed to dim to darkness in the room, the phone illuminated by a spotlight, its shadows casting a menacing illusion that loomed mightily over his head, taunting him. He reached for the receiver, and everything seemed to go back to normal. He had easily retrieved her number from the local White Pages, but he wondered if their chance encounters downtown would be enough for Laura to know who he was. He hoped – oh, how desperately he hoped – that it would not seem too bold.

Three rings? Is she screening her calls? This was a bad idea. She's going to think I'm a creep. I'm too old for her.

"Hello?"

"Hi... uh, may I please speak to Laura?"

"This is she."

"Oh. Hi, Laura." He worried that he sounded too familiar. They weren't friends, after all, merely acquaintances. "This is Gavin Prior."

"Hello, Mr. Prior. How are you today?"

"Gavin is fine." He tried to smile when he said it, but he wasn't sure she would catch his meaning.

"Gavin then."

And so, the conversation didn't go nearly as badly as Gavin had convinced himself it would. She was very friendly, even more friendly than he would have imagined considering the odd circumstances of the call. To his delight, she agreed to a dinner later that week. The smile happened automatically, wide and true. It was one of those smiles that you simply cannot control and don't realize is happening until you feel your muscles in your face straining to maintain what your heart dictates you must display for the world to see.

The front door opened silently.

"Hey, Dad." Tanner was home. Gavin turned to look at him, smiling like Tanner could only remember from his childhood. "Whoa! What's going on with you?" His dad seldom smiled at all, and never like Alice's Cheshire cat. He was taken completely aback.

"Tanner, it would appear," he paused and gulped a bit, "that your father has a date." He put his arms out as if to say "Ta Da!"

Tanner was speechless for a moment, his eyebrows raised in disbelief. The he managed to mutter, "You're kidding me."

"Tanner, you know I don't joke." It was almost funny, but it was actually very true.

"Dad... I..." He struggled to find the words, finally looking at his father genuinely pleased and said, "I'm happy for you, Dad."

Gavin smiled. Though the silence was long enough to be awkward, he took in the moment, enjoying the first real connection with his son since Tanner was a little boy. His life was beginning to turn around.

PART FOUR

Laura and Mary

"This is she."

"Oh. Hi, Laura. This is Gavin Prior."

"Hello, Mr. Prior. How are you today?"

"Gavin is fine."

Well, isn't he a friendly one? "Gavin then."

"I am doing well, though wishing the skies would clear up."

"Ah, yes, I agree with you there. What can I help you with today?" She sounded like she was at work.

"Well, Laura, I was actually wondering if I might ask you a question."

"Go on."

"I was wondering if perhaps you might be interested in going out to dinner sometime."

Was this really happening? Was she being asked on a date? She had stopped crying about Joseph a week before and had finally resigned herself to the fact that her fantasy with him was forever gone, but a date so soon was strange, especially after ten years of a love life more barren than the Serengeti. What fortunate timing, she mused, but she also wondered if she was ready to open herself to someone new just yet.

"Oh, Gavin... oh, I don't know. That is so kind of you."

"It wouldn't be anything big or fancy." He sounded nervous, which was cute, "I would just like to get to know you better, if that's not too bold of me."

"Oh, not at all. It's just..." She never considered dating Gavin Prior. Everyone knew him as the widower. Now that she considered it, he was extremely handsome, and only a couple of years her senior. In fact, considering their respective stories (or what she knew of his through the grapevine), it would make sense for them to date.

"Just what?"

Oh, why the hell not. "I would love to go to dinner. Though ONLY dinner." She had to be careful, having coming out of a difficult time so recently. The last thing she needed was another misunderstanding leading to another evening ending with "So, are we gonna bang or what?"

"Only dinner."

"It's a date then."

"I'll call you later this week, and we can pick a restaurant."

"Sounds great."

"Goodbye, Laura."

"Talk to you later, Gavin." She hung up the phone and stood there, smiling to herself. She was nervous about the whole situation and still not sure if she should be going on a date so soon, but it pleased her, empowered her somehow. Mary was sitting at the counter across the kitchen, looking up with raised eyebrows at her mother.

"And what was that all about?" She had heard enough to assume, but not enough to be sure.

"That was Gavin Prior. We are... well, I think we are going out to dinner this week."

"Really? Mom, that's so great!" They had gotten closer since Laura had stopped drinking weeks before. They really talked now, especially since Mary had been such a mature and much needed support after Joseph's visit.

"I'm just not sure if it's wise." She looked up to the ceiling, considering.

"Mom, I know it seems soon since so much happened so recently, but if you think about it, it's really been over ten years at this point. I think it's time. If you are unsure, just take it slow." She didn't have social skills, but she was still wise for her years.

"Yes, you're right. That is, I am hoping it works. He sure is a handsome fellow."

"Yuck."

"What? What's wrong with Gavin Prior? He's better looking than your father!"

"I guess. But he's just so... old."

"Mary Augustine! He isn't even fifty! You kids..." She smiled and shook her head. "What about you, young lady. Isn't there anyone you can see yourself dating in the future?"

Boy talk. How sitcom.

"I don't know, Mom... maybe." She blushed. Whenever the

two would watch television together on weeknights, they would often make comments about the sillyness of inevitable mother/daughter boy talk. It was one of the few times that Laura paid full attention to her daughter, and one of the few things they did together that they still enjoyed. Laura would look over at Mary and imitate the melodramatic delivery.

"Mary, you are... you are..." She paused and looked over her shoulder, hair falling across her face. "Pregnant?" She would put her hand up to her mouth in mock surprise.

"Mother, I knew you would be mad! This is why I didn't tell you! I hate you! I hate you, Mom!" Mary would yell in return, shaking her fists up and down.

"But... do you love him?" Laura would drop her voice an octave for the word "love," making it sound more like "luuhve" to add to the drama. Now that they were having a real boy talk for the first time, though, it was significantly less entertaining.

Laura knew that Mary had a thing for George Rutherford, though she wished she didn't The boy – no, the man – was much too old for her. Granted, he did seem immature for his age, which would make for an illusion of compatibility, but Laura knew it was a formula for a bad situation. Still, Mary hardly socialized with anyone, so she didn't forbid their interactions. She only hoped that she would learn what she could from the boy and hopefully move on to someone her own age for romantic endeavors. For the moment, she just hoped that the romance was staying at unmentioned feelings rather than actual actions. She shuddered at the thought.

"Well, maybe you could go on a date with the Prior boy," Laura suggested. Mary rolled her eyes in response and turned back to her paper. Her mother wouldn't let up. "Well, have you thought about dating at all?"

"Of course I've thought about it, Mom. I'm eighteen." Mary paused with her eyebrows raised and mouth open, searching for the words. "I just... well, I just haven't found anyone worth my time – yet." The way she said it made it seem like she had someone in mind. The pause was a little too casual to be natural, the inflection a bit too forced. Laura didn't want to think about her daughter with a washed-up townie. She dreamed of her being swept away by a doctor or lawyer from some other magical place where dreams always come true and the marriage is perfect and the house is immaculate and the grandchildren are always beautiful and perfectly happy – the stuff of every American mother's dreams for their daughters.

George

The wind whipped through the empty stairwell, giving George a welcome respite from the heat. It was unusually warm, despite it being late at night. A heat wave was plaguing northern Massachusetts following recent weeks of rain. The moisture that the rainy weeks had left behind made for an uncomfortable humidity, and a breeze of any kind was welcomed with open arms.

George checked his watch. He had never been stood up before, especially by a customer. Granted, his usual clientelle weren't always punctual, but Elijah, one of his regulars, was almost an hour late at this point. Timidly, George stepped out of the neglected groundskeeper building and looked out into the woods, straining his eyes to see into the darkness. With the light coming from behind him, however, it was nearly impossible to see anything but the immediate surroundings of the building. The contrast in light did not allow his eyes to properly adjust to the darkness.

George had finally saved enough money for what he estimated would be reasonable expenses for moving back to New York City. He considered the costs of renting a truck, food, utilities, and rent until he found a job, as well as weekend entertainment, all while assuming a comfortable lifestyle in the West Village. He had yet to decide when he would make the big move; it was too tempting not to pad his accounts a bit more before he left, especially when the money was coming so easily. With this in mind, he decided to abandon the night's sale.

It took a few moments before he was able to see where he was walking, the path to the groundskeeper building lacking any form of illumination. Due to the overgrowth, he was forced to move very slowly so as not to trip on a forgotten branch or overgrown root. Like a camera coming into focus, his eyes eventually adapted, and he was able to make it out of the woods, across the field, and back to his car in a reasonable amount of time. Doing the calculations in his head, he figured he had enough time to get home and watch the first Lord of the Rings film before the sun rose to greet the new day.

The drive home was quiet. George preferred to drive in silence late into the night in order to keep his attention on the road. Whenever he turned his iPod on in the car, he was prone to drifting in and out of sleep, a very dangerous habit. Despite the business he was running, he was still a cautious man.

When he arrived home, he stepped out of his car and

walked across the gravel driveway, each step a crunch that broke through the silence of the night. He looked around and tried to make out any potential shapes in the darkness surrounding his building. He had been as jumpy as ever lately, his paranoia ever growing. He walked down the concrete stairs that led to his basement apartment and shoved the door open. At first, the door wouldn't cooperate, but with an extra slam of the shoulder, it finally complied and allowed him to enter his home.

He wasn't a complete slob, though his apartment was anything but clean. There were clothes littering the floor and more emptied glasses around the couch and coffee table than one person could ever use. When he turned on the overhead light, it was clear that this apartment was generally bathed in darkness, except for the blue glow of the television. It was that harsh white light that reminded him not of home but of a hospital or other commercial building – the type of light that anyone in their right mind would replace with a table or floor lamp sporting the warmth of a soft white incandescent bulb. George, however, hardly ever had the lights on anyway, so the temporarily harsh light was tolerable.

He walked over to the kitchenette and put his keys on the linoleum countertop. After grabbing a sugary non-diet soda from the refrigerator, he walked over to his stack of DVDs and squatted down, resting on the balls of his feet, to browse the titles for the night's entertainment. He settled on the first Lord of the Rings movie, as originally planned. "My precious," he muttered with a grin as he put the DVD into the player.

After downing half the bottle of soda and processing the

main federal warnings of the DVD, George realized with mock terror that he was consuming large amounts of sugar and caffeine at well past midnight. With a shrug of his shoulders and roll of his eyes, he pulled out his cellphone to scroll through the contacts list, searching for others that might be awake at such a late hour. Despite knowing exactly who was in his contacts, he felt the innane neccessity of going through the entire list before he made a call. In the end, just as he expected, he called up his business supplier, Mike, and invited him to join him in a night of cinematic fantasy adventure.

Half an hour later, Mike walked through the unlocked front door of George's apartment and helped himself to the kitchen, simply offering a "Hey, man." Mike was still not one for manners.

"Hey yourself. What's going on?"

"Same shit, different day." Their conversations weren't very enlightening. Mike sat on the opposite end of the couch and let his eyes glaze over as the film began. The Lord of the Rings movies were one of the highest forms of modern art as far as George was concerned, but regardless of his opinion, the first hour of its inaugural film was unquestionably slow. As such, George tried to make conversation.

"Got stood up today."

"By a noob?" Mike called new customers "noobs," short for newbie or "n-0-0-b" as he would type in his online chat windows.

"No. One of my regs."

"Who?"

"That movie guy, Hart."

"That's weird, but sometimes the older ones get caught up with family or other shit like that. You still got his stuff?"

"What?"

"You got his stuff? It would make this movie ten times better."

George had never considered doing the drugs that he distributed among the residents of Ipswich. Ever since his failure in New York, he had a bad taste in his mouth on the entire subject, and he considered himself to be in the business solely for the purpose of getting back on his feet. Still, it wasn't like they would be doing anything unhealthy. And he did get stood up. And this movie was boring, art or not.

"Fine."

Several minutes later, George's basement apartment was in a haze. It was at this point that the decision was made that finally tipped the scale. While they were completely mellow and would have been fine melting into the couch and appreciating every flower and blade of grass in Middle Earth like it was the highest form of elightenment, it was George's wonderful idea to start drinking.

"Let's drink," he had said.

They only had liquor, but they didn't think it was a problem because Mike brought mixers. How lucky to have a friend who was always prepared! It was downhill from there, the crossfading effects of the two mind altering substances making them sloppy. They stumbled, they laughed, they put on music while the TV was still on, making a undistinguishable blend of sounds, and finally, the insatiable munchies kicked in. They ate everything in sight – chips, pretzels, bread, pickles, butter (by itself), ketchup, and more chips. They were gourmets, the new Julia Childs of the world! Wondering why no one had ever thought of a mayonaise and Twinkie combination before, it was Mike who suddenly was struck by inspiration.

"North Street Diner."

"W-what?" George asked, giggly.

"Let's go to North Street Diner, in Boston."

"Oh my God, yes!" It was the only twenty-four-hour diner they could think of, and they had no concept of it being an hour away by car. They were immune to time. Thankfully, Mike had not drank as much as George, and his considerably more substantial body weight meant he was merely buzzed by the alcohol they consumed. Still, it was a miracle they made it down Route 95 without incident. They came very close to veering off the road several times when Mike started giggling at the jokes George was making regarding the intoxicated insights about the concept of time and space, but they made it alive nevertheless.

They stumbled into the diner laughing obnoxiously and falling over everything in their paths. The waiter looked up, not surprised. Boston was a college town, and he was used to drunks and stoners coming in at all hours of the day. The two took a booth by the window and started browsing the colorfully printed menus.

"Dude, what are you getting?" George asked without giving Mike enough time for even a sober person to decide.

"I just want everything. It all looks so good." They decided to each order their own sampler platters, complete with a side of ranch dressing for dipping. Each bite was an explosion of flavor and pleasure. Though they were both starting to come down from the effects of the drugs, they both finished their plates quite completely. When the waiter brought the bill, George reached for his wallet, only to discover it was not in his pocket. Shit! I left it on the counter, he remembered, not that it mattered much because it was empty as it was, and wouldn't have been much of a help. As he was considering how to awkwardly ask Mike to cover his portion, he remembered the wad of cash in his back pocket. Technically, it was the payment that he was supposed to be giving Mike the next day, but he could stall until he found the money to replace it. It was a day away, and he didn't have to worry about it. He pulled out a twenty that wasn't his and put it on the table.

Even though he was coming down, George was exhilirated by the adventure. It was more exciting than anything he had done in years. He looked over at Mike, who had a glimmer in his eye.

"You tired, Georgey?" he asked mischeviously.

"No. Why?"

"You have to be up for anything tomorrow?"

"Nope."

"Then how would you like to take a little trip to Pleasureville, USA?" In Mike's hand was a baggy filled with crushed white powder worth more than its weight in gold to the two men. George considered it. A year before, his decision would have been different.

"Let's do it."

Tanner

Tanner stared at the torn canvas, his forearms dripping in fresh red, yellow, and burnt sienna. He had been painting ferociously, letting all his frustration escape him as he worked on the abstract portrait, splashing bold lines across the blank slate, creating the outline of a person with a round face but strong features. Conceptual at most, his creation met a quick end as one too many rough strokes sent his brush piercing through the canvas and his arm following it, carrying too much momentum to stop at such a surprise. His arm followed through, widening the hole and soaking his arm in the paint that had been so recently applied. He stood catching his breath as he stared and considered how he had let himself get so excited.

It was mostly frustration with himself. He had been thinking about Timothy without pause ever since his freaking weird run-in with that Perran character in Maudson Park. He told himself that Perran was crazy but followed such ideas with thoughts about how he missed Timothy, his bright eyes, and his charming smile. No, no, no! he told himself. It isn't right. It was his best buddy he was thinking about. I'm an athlete, he reasoned. I shouldn't be thinking like that.

Still, they wouldn't go away. He had even dreamed about spending one of the recent perfect summer days with him. It was all so unbelievable. He considered that these bizarre feelings had somehow possibly always been lurking deep down, but their friendly comraderie and intimacy (the friendship kind, of course) had masked them and made them feel normal. But he didn't know if they were normal or not, and the confusion built up until he exploded, tearing the canvas and covering himself with paint in the process, panting in frustration in his attic bedroom that on a summer night.

The water was warm as he slowly washed the paint off in the bathroom attached to his bedroom. He closed his eyes and let the water calm him. He forced his thoughts away from the situation that plagued him. School was over, and never again would he have to suffer through a high school class. Only college awaited him in the future – four years at Northeastern University in downtown Boston, playing for their soccer team and studying business. It was cliche, but he was looking forward to it. He had heard that they had recently built a new art gallery in the Student Center and was secretly harboring hopes that he would be able to fit an art class or two into his schedule. He began to wonder for a moment if Timothy would visit but stopped himself abruptly. No, no… what else? Dad's got a date. God, that's weird. He didn't know much about the Augustine family, but it seemed his father was infatuated with the woman. She was pretty enough for an older woman, Tanner considered, and he supposed it wouldn't hurt to be happy for his father. It was unusual but nice to be able to have actual conversations with the old man. He just wished he was in any sort of mood to be having a conversation. If only things could go back to how they were.

He was staring himself down in the mirror, hands dripping wet, silent except for the rumbling of the old pipes somewhere in the house, when the phone rang in his bedroom. Suddenly hoping it might be his best friend, he bounded over into his room, pounding his feet against the original wood floors. He picked up the phone with still-wet hands.

"Hello?"

"Call him, Prior." It wasn't Timothy.

"Excuse me?"

"Just call him."

"Perran?"

Silence. The stranger hung up the phone. Tanner slowly put the phone back in its cradle. He stared at the phone sitting atop its old end table home. Who does that guy think he is? He doesn't understand the situation at all, Tanner thought. But maybe he did. Maybe he was just trying to help. Still, it is difficult for a teenage boy to face the truth sometimes, especially when it means admitting to something... well, something like this.

The phone sat there, taunting him. He hadn't talked to Timothy in over a week. It was past the point of being angry because of a fight or argument, past the point of blaming stubborn teenage hormones. Presently, it was just painful. He felt like he was missing his arm, his other half. They had been together in some capacity since they were kids. He decided he couldn't let these feelings he was having – whatever they were – get in the way of them continuing their lives. They needed to solve the issue, to move forward somehow. He hesitantly reached for the phone.

Boy, the dial tone was loud. Does that mean anything? Tanner thought that might mean something. He fiddled with the volume controls on the side of the phone. Couldn't too loud a dial tone might mess up the call somehow? Of all the calls he had made in his life, he couldn't risk messing this one up. He was nervous. Pausing before hitting the last number in Timothy's cellphone number, he took a deep breath. Then, he let his finger dial the last 2. After two rings, Timothy picked up.

"Tanner?"

"Hey, Timothy."

Awkward pause.

"Hey."

"Hey, listen... we should talk."

"Yeah, that's a good idea. I really need to get some stuff off my chest." Another pause. "You mind if I come over?"

"I'll be upstairs."

"See you in a few."

Click.

It ended up being much easier than Tanner had originally expected. There was no yelling or swearing or embarassing admissions of anything, and relief poured over him in waves as he thought it was over and that everything would be back to normal. Almost immediately, however, he realized that he still had a confrontation awaiting him, minutes away. He started to sweat, hands clammy. Just breathe, Tanner, he told himself. Everything will be okay.

Mary and George

As she stared at the filtered yellow glow of the light, turntable humming with a struggling motor, Mary wondered if microwaves really did cause cancer. With the first couple of pops, her worries melted away like butter as the smell of popcorn filtered out through the radiation-leaking cracks in the machine and into the kitchen. She had a variety of sodas stocked in the fridge and was awaiting George's arrival for their movie date. She wasn't as much nervous as she was hesitantly optimistic. She and George had a nice friendship and always had good conversation, so she wasn't worried about it being awkward. Moreso, she was curious as to what would come of it. She had always thought of George as cute in a sort of aged puppy way, but she wasn't sure what he thought of her. The makeup she was wearing from her long neglected birthday present the winter before was evidence that she wanted to remind George that she was a lady in addition to being his friend.

Thankfully, her mother was out on a date with Gavin Prior, the widower and former recluse from the northside of town. She wasn't expecting any prurient activity to be on the agenda, but she knew her mother would have been very awkward about the situation, especially considering the age difference between Mary and George. Mary wondered how her mother's date would go, briefly entertaining the fantasy of becoming part of a wealthy family on the northside. As she briefly daydreamed, she wiped down the counter and double checked to make sure everything was presentable for her guest.

There was a faint knock on the door, which Mary found cute, assuming George was nervous. When she opened the door, she did her best not to show her surprise. George was standing, his clothes sloppy and unwashed, and his eyes with big bags under them. He looked gaunt, like the image of the George she knew sloppily pulled over a skeleton without enough stuffing underneath.

"H-hey, George." She was hesitant.

"Yo."

"Come in." She stood aside and put her arm out to her side to motion for him to join her in the house. He lazily took a step inside. "You look... uh... tired."

"Yeah, I was out pretty late last night," he said. "Crazy shit, man."

Mary was confused. She had never seen George like this before, acting as if he were on some sort of drugs. She tried to convince herself that it was not the case and that he simply stayed awake much too late the night before. Still, his language and sentence structure said otherwise. For the first time, Mary saw him as a man, and it frightened her.

"Can I get you anything to drink?" she asked, a bit too eagerly.

"Coke." George paused, then thought about his answer and found it humorous. "Heh."

So, that's it. He's on drugs, Mary thought to herself with exasperation. George would never find a drug joke funny before, let alone laugh at himself like an idiot. Mary wondered with disappoinment what her friend was letting himself become. She showed him to the living room, where he collapsed on the couch and seemed to sink into the cushions. Her heart sunk, expectations falling for the evening like a dead autumn leaf lazily drifting to the ground. She couldn't believe things were going so poorly already.

"So, what are we watching?" he asked, putting his hand out for the bowl of popcorn she was bringing over for them to share. He put it on the couch next to his leg. A vibrating noise came from his pants before she could answer, and he pulled out his cellphone. After reading a text message that arrived, he looked slightly nervous, "Hey, Mar, you don't know who Mike Cassidy is, do you?"

"No. I haven't heard of him," she said, pulling out a DVD with the Movie Express sticker on the front. "We're watching Canadian Vampire."

"So, uh, he wouldn't know where you live, would he?"

"No. I've never met the guy."

George looked relieved, then asked, "Do you have any aspirin?" Mary rolled her eyes. He had been there not even five minutes, and she was already annoyed. Where was the charming George Rutherford she knew? Normally, he would be cute and look young for his age, his big brown eyes lighting up with excitement as he told her about a new movie or story he had read, a new film adaptation of a favorite classic being released – anything about his many passions. Now, he just seemed burnt out and messy. She walked over to the bathroom and rummaged around in the medicine cabinet before coming up empty handed.

"Sorry. We must have run out, George." She didn't really know what to do. What should have been at best a budding romance and at worst a friendly get-together was turning into an awkward and disappointing bore.

"Shit. My head hurts." George rubbed his eyes. Mary had never heard him swear before, not once. Mary decided she didn't really want to sit in her living room with this disappointing shell of her friend for two or three hours while she grew more and more frustrated with the situation.

"Listen, George, do you want to take a raincheck? You don't seem to be feeling so great, and we can always do this another time."

He looked up at her without lifting his head, moving only his bloodshot eyes. He tried to look thankful, conerned even, but he only looked annoyed, "I think that's probably a good idea. Help me up?" He put his hand out for her to assist him to stand. It was getting ridiculous. She pulled him up, noticed he smelled, and guided him back to the front door. As he shuffled out and down the driveway, she shouted after him.

"Go get some sleep, George!" She didn't want to lose her friend, but it appeared she had no choice. It seemed the deed was already done.

Looking around at all the preparations she had made, Mary pursed her lips and thought. She shouldn't have to deal with such nonsense. Granted, George helped her emerge from her shell, but she had done a lot of social growing on her own, George was simply interested in the same things she was – or at least he used to be. If he wanted to delve into the underbelly of society and lose himself to his own self-pity, then he could do it alone. Pleased with the conclusions she had come to, she nodded to herself once and walked up to her room.

She felt strangely empowered and decided to work on the application for University of Massachusetts. College had never been in her plans before, but she had stumbled across the English Education program in a brochure the institution left at her high school and had taken the application just in case. Presently, she felt like she had the world to offer the university and would be accepted with the highest of scholarships. It gave her something else to think about, something productive. She walked over to her desk at clicked on the lamp. Sighing and letting go of the disappointments of the day, she put her pen to the paper and began to work.

Elijah

The foul smell of burning rubber went unnoticed as the black Escalade screeched to a halt. With its tinted windows, the people inside were completely masked in anonymity. That is, of course, until the doors swept open, casting a slight breeze across Elijah Hart's face. He noticed through squinted, dry eyes that all the men were wearing identical windbreakers with the letters DEA emblazoned on the front and back. It took a moment due to the THC running through his system, but as soon as he realized who the men in dark jackets were, Elijah's heart skipped a beat. They surrounded him in rehearsed precision.

"Elijah Hart, you're going to have to come with us," one of the identical men said. Elijah wasn't sure which, but it didn't matter. His fear kept him rooted to the ground, unable to move. The men took several quick steps and firmly secured their target by the crooks of his arms, dragging him (albeit painlessly) to the vehicle from where they had erupted. Elijah's brain would not function. He was running through excuses and alibis, his ears turning red and his hands getting clammy. He was suddenly aware of how fast his heart was beating.

With a bang, the door of the Escalade slammed shut, and Elijah was sitting in the darkness of the vehicle, flanked on either side by two of the strong looking men. His thoughts turned to his family, his two darling daughters, and what they would do without him, for he had convinced himself in his altered state that he was being driven to his execution. He thought of his small business as the car traversed the bumpy road that led to the highway, and for a moment he remembered his employees that would be unable to function without his knowledge of the store. If the store failed, his family would be in a great deal of debt. His wife and daughters would be footing the bill for his illegal habit.

Just as his eyes were beginning to adjust to the darkness inside the vehicle, he noticed that the driver pulled into a parking spot much more quickly than seemed necessary. White sunlight flooded the car, blinding him as they opened the doors and pushed him out and onto the asphalt. He was led toward a stark grey building surrounded entirely by trees. He had no idea where he was, though he wagered it probably was not more than thirty minutes outside of Ipswich.

If there was anything that Elijah had learned from managing a video rental store, it was that the movies were nothing like real life. As such, he was very surprised when he was led into an interrogation room that looked exactly like something out of a prime-time crime drama, lazily swinging overhead lamp and all.

The robotic drones started by asking him background questions about his life: his name, basic biographical information, simple things to warm him up to the process. After asking him about his maternal grandmother's childhood town, they took a black and white photograph out of a crisp manilla file folder and pushed it in front of him. Elijah was faced with the portrait of a young overweight man. Curly dark hair rested above beady brown eyes that fell slightly too close together. It was a face he had never seen before and had no real desire to see in real life. For the first time, he was confused as to whether or not the agents had really been looking for him at all. He doubted, however slightly, that they had found the right man.

"Do you know this person?" the man on the left asked in a deep baritone. Elijah answered with complete honesty.

"I have never seen him in my life, sir." The man pounded his fist on the table in frustration. His colleague leaned over and whispered something into his ear as he nodded in acknowledgment. He tried another tactic.

"Do you know one Mr. Michael Cassidy, Mr. Hart?"

"Honestly, sir, I have no idea what you are talking about." The pleading nature of his voice was a testament to the truth of his words.

"Are you aware, Mr. Hart, that Michael Cassidy is the biggest coke dealer in the Cape Ann region? Are you aware what kind of sentence goes along with associating yourself with such a man?" These men were serious, though Elijah truly knew nothing about what they were talking about.

"Honestly, I don't know the man. It's possible I may have heard the name once, but I truly don't think I have." By now, he was holding back tears.

"Well, Hart, I don't know what you want us to do. We have video evidence implicating you in some serious crimes connected to this man, and unless you want to lose your house and your business, you'd better start talking. You give us some information we can use, and we'll let you go." He spread his hands, palms up, in his final offer. Elijah considered it for a moment. He had some information that would be of interest to the Drug Enforcement Agency, but it was an unwritten rule that such information couldn't be shared. He could never look George in the eye again if he shared this information, and that was assuming that he didn't send someone after him to threaten him... or worse. Still, his family was on the line.

There was no option.

"Well," he said, "there is someone..." and he began to talk.

Gavin and Laura

Nothing is more surprising than seeing a face in the mirror that is not your own. Its eyes follow yours, its movements are identical, when you gasp, it gasps, but for the life of you, it is unrecognizable. You consider the possibility of an intruder, a demonic possession, but it gradually dawns on you that it is, in fact and without a doubt, an image of you being reflected, and no one else. Such was the experience Laura Augustine had as she observed herself in the mirror with make up and jewelery formal enough for a first date for the first time in over a lonely decade of pathetically pining after someone not worth it. There were a few new lines creasing her face with the memories of experience and age, but also a previously absent glow of anticipation and spirit that had been missing from her features for years.

It had taken her two hours to finish preparing for her date

with Gavin. She spent thirty minutes alone in front of the closet deciding what to wear, and the shoes to match were a whole other story. She wasn't the type of woman to be particularly picky (she never had been) but was simply nervous and unsure of herself. She was worried about what to say and do, what mannerisms to use. God, she thought, how can I be this rusty? I am a grown woman!

She walked over to her nightstand where a pair of long forgotten earrings lay covered in dust. She brushed them off with her fingers and held them up to her face, pursing her lips in her best Vogue face as she observed herself in the mirror. They would have to do. They were her nicest earrings. She had been told by a nameless ex-husband that the green stones in the particular set of earrings she was holding brought out her eyes. She hoped that Gavin would notice such things and had been growing ever more optimistic about the prospect of a date for several days. Gavin had called earlier in the day to confirm their plans, and when she picked up the phone, she immediately became nervous, butterflies flapping around in her stomach in excitement. To be young again! She was glowing with youthful energy that everyone around her had thought been permanently extinguished.

The phone rang. She shuffled over quickly – the way older women always shuffle when they are afraid of getting a run in their stockings before a big event. She picked up the receiver, holding it slightly away from her cheek so as not to ruin her makeup.

"Hello?"

"Hi, Laura, it's Gavin. Just wanted to make sure it's okay if I pick you up in about ten minutes." How thoughtful, making she sure was ready in time.

"Yes, Gavin, that would be perfect." She hung up the phone and started running around, putting the finishing touches on her makeup and outfit, moving as if the fast forward button had been pushed on her life's remote. Her nerves started to act up again, her hands getting cold as she doubted whether or not she was ready to be going on a date.

When she walked downstairs, she saw Mary coming in the front door with several reusable tote bags in her arms. She hadn't even realized her daughter had left earlier. She had been too preoccupied with preparing for her date.

"What is that you have there?"

"Oh, just some soda and popcorn and stuff," Mary blushed. "I think I'm just going to stay in and watch a movie or something tonight, and we didn't have any snacks."

Sure she was. Laura knew that look. She had been a teenager once herself. Whether Mary was having a party or having a boy over, she didn't put much thought into it. She knew her daughter was, on the whole, a responsible young woman, and she was frankly too preoccupied with her date to put much thought to the issue.

Walking to the front door, she straightened her hair and made sure her dress was hanging properly on her shoulders. She glanced out the thin window in the front door and saw a dark green SUV turning the corner onto the street. Immediately, her heart began to beat faster, and small beads of sweat appeared on her skin. Gavin exited the car. He looked very handsome and put together, sporting a blue button-up shirt and dark pants. The most surprising part of the outfit was that it all actually fit, showing off his broad shoulders and trim waist and giving him an aura of confidence that was often lost among many American males who fell victim to oversized clothes.

He knocked.

Laura opened the door slightly too eagerly and with a bit too much faux surprise, but Gavin found it all irresistably endearing.

"Hi there." His hair was parted to the side, perfectly groomed. "You look absolutely stunning tonight, if you don't mind my saying so."

Laura blushed. It had been years since she had felt the warmth of a compliment. "Why, thank you. You don't look half bad yourself. Shall we go?"

"After you," he said, extending his arm out toward his car. Mary watched from the living room and called out as her mother was walking out the door.

"Have fun, Mom!"

Laura looked back and smiled but didn't say anything. She simply raised her eyebrows in a here-goes-nothing fashion and closed the door gently behind her.

While she was sitting in the passenger seat of Gavin's car as they turned onto High Street, Laura noted that there should be a left arm rest for the passengers who are on first dates and don't know where to put their arms without looking like they are asking for their hands to be held. She made a mental note to patent the idea. To solve her conundrum, she rested both hands on top of her purse, which lay in her lap. It matched her dress perfectly.

Their conversation wasn't uncomfortable but had the air that all first-date conversations generally do. There were the introductory questions that must be asked in order to get a good mental image of the person but that are almost impossible to ask in natural conversation. Nevertheless, they talked about their jobs, their children, where they grew up, and despite being introductory, were both enthralled with the other's answers the entire time. Laura cracked jokes about Gavin living on the northside, as the class rivalry was as common a topic in Ipswich as the weather, but he brushed it off with a laugh, removing himself from the attitude that was associated with his neighborhood. He appreciated that Laura had some spunk to her, and Laura was relieved to see he was not pompous. They were only entering Route 95, but so far, things were going well.

The inside of Gavin's car was impeccably clean. Laura wondered whether it was always spotless or if he had prepared it specifically for their date. The black dashboard had a new-car shine and smell, despite it clearly being an older model car. Not a single crumb was in the corners of the cup holders or crevices of the seats. She knew without looking that there were no loose change, bottle caps, or wrappers forgotten on the floor or under where she sat. She glanced over at the odometer to assure herself that the car was well used, and it read a healthy 80,000 miles. Gavin smiled over, thinking she was looking at him.

"So, I hope you like Cuban. This place just opened in Georgetown, and I've heard it's fantastic," Gavin said, finally guiding the conversation past introductions and into more casual subjects.

"There isn't a type of food I don't like, so I don't think you have to worry about me." She wondered if she should seem more picky. She had forgotten the rules of playing hard to get.

"That's good to hear. I appreciate when people are open minded."

At first, Laura thought it was a gunshot. In retrospect, there is little circumstance that would be cause for a gunshot on the multi-lane interstate highway. Immediately, the car jerked down and to the side. In that moment, she grabbed the ceiling handle for support as she looked over in horror and saw Gavin's muscles straining as he struggled to keep the car stable, braking quickly and pulling over to the curb. Cars flew past as Laura caught her breath, and Gavin put his hand protectively on her arm.

"Are you okay?" he asked, shaken but not distressed. She took a moment to find the words, both startled by the popped tire and distracted by the human contact.

"Yes, yes… I think I'm fine." She manually slowed her breathing.

Gavin opened the driver's side door when a lull in the highway traffic allowed it and stepped around to let Laura out of the vehicle. Putting a hand up for her to hold, he helped her step out.

"Ever change a tire before?" It was more rhetorical than a serious request. He rolled his sleeves up in preparation.

"I actually have not. Would you mind if I helped? I probably should know how, just in case." Gavin at first looked puzzled by her request. He wasn't actually asking her to help, though he wouldn't mind teaching her.

"You are all dressed up. Wouldn't you be worried about ruining your dress?" To her delight, he was concerned and not in the least bit condescending.

"It'll be fine."

"Really, I can take care of it in just a minute." He was uncomfortable with Laura wanting to help but couldn't help but be intrigued by her desire to be involved.

"I want to help."

"Okay." He was hesitant but agreed to let her assist him with the repair. Gavin went to the back of his SUV and opened the hatch. Inside, he pulled out the floor of the trunk, revealing a spare tire and the required tools. He handed the small box of Allen wrenches to Laura. "Here, take this back to the flat." She smiled as she took the box. She was intrigued by the man and was glad that he was willing to let her help. Any fellow that she pursued romantically would have to look at the relationship as a partnership. After the fiasco she had been through with Joseph, she would accept nothing less. Gavin lumbered over carrying the tire, which was the same size as the other tires, unlike the spare donut types Laura was used to seeing. She noticed that he was still in very good shape for a man of forty-seven. His veins stuck out in his arms as he carried the awkward object over.

"So, what do we do now?" Laura asked, pulling her dress up to her knees so she could crouch down by the tire that had turned into more of a collection of rubber fragments.

"Well, first we have to lift up the car on the jack."

Gavin walked Laura through the steps of changing a tire for the first time in her life. Being a gentleman, he insisted on doing most of the actual work, but he allowed Laura at her request to be involved. He was kind and jovial as he told her exactly what he was doing and why, and she happily handed him tools and held the lug nuts to keep them from being misplaced. They laughed and joked, lightly poking fun at each other. By the end of the process, they both wore big smiles as the chemistry between them had replaced any of the previous stress or surprise of the dangerous situation.

The blooming lovers eventually made it to their dinner, albeit forty-five minutes late. Thankfully, it was not crowded, and they were able to be sit down soon after their arrival. Their conversation continued to flow even easier than before, and an hour and half after they sat down, they leaned back from empty plates laughing heartily at each other's jokes, well fed and happy for the first time in many years. Laura looked over to Gavin and smiled as she took the moment in. The candle flickered and cast a warm light upon the kind man's face. She thought of her perceptions – of everyone's perceptions – of the man before her, the town widower. He had been known as a recluse, although kind, and here he was treating her to a magnificent night out simply out of the goodness of his heart. There was more to Gavin Prior than people knew, and she was filled with a warm desire to explore and grow with him. Gavin smiled back happy just to be in Laura's presence.

Hours later, Gavin pulled into the driveway at Laura's home. He turned the car off with a twist of the key, letting the rumbling engine putter to silence. Walking around the car, he opened Laura's door for her and again helped her out of the large vehicle. They walked arm in arm to her front door. All the lights were off in the house except for a yellow beam coming from Mary's room on the second floor. Under the porch light that was beginning to attract the summertime mosquitoes, Gavin gently turned Laura to face him.

"Laura, I had..." He paused to find the right words. "I had an absolutely fantastic time tonight. I hope I will see you again?" He phrased it like a question, which Laura found cute. It was obvious that there was going to be another date. The two who had such trouble moving on and connecting with others were finally going to do just that – together. To seal the deal, Gavin produced a sunflower, unconventional but equally romantic, and presented it to his date, though for the life of her, Laura couldn't figure out from where.

"Of course, Gavin. Of course there will be another date." A big smile spread across her face. "And soon, I hope."

Gavin leaned in and gave Laura a tasteful peck on the lips that sent a shock of warmth between them both. They both knew they were making too much progress to risk physicality that night. They had agreed to take things slow and would not give in to temptation, no matter how strong it was, and it WAS strong.

Laura said nothing but kept beaming as she turned around and walked into her house, closing the door gently behind her with a newfound bounce in her step. Gavin put his hands in his pockets and, smiling uncontrollably, walked back to his car. He drove home under the ink black sky in the light of the crescent moon, happier than he had been in years.

Ensemble

The light of a fresh bulb flickered to life, illuminating the exposed ceiling beams in Tanner's attic bedroom. His antique desk was ruined with paint splatters and was slowly developing a thin layer of dust while his bed across the room was unkempt and unmade. Tanner was oblivious to these things as he paced his room nervously awaiting Timothy's arrival.

He wasn't sure if he was ready to see his friend again. Perran was right though. It had to be done. Timothy was too important to drop by the wayside because of whatever weird feelings Tanner was experiencing. He would still be his friend in the end, even if it was awkward for a bit. Tanner could handle awkward if it meant having him back in his life.

He considered his options. On the one hand, he could apologize for the misunderstanding and hope that things could go back to the way they were. This would leave feelings unattended but seemed to be the cleanest option. He would just have to bury the unthinkable things he thought about his friend. On the other hand, however, he could admit the feelings that he was just starting to admit to himself. Timothy could very well be understanding and maybe even feel similarly. This seems highly unlikely, though, Tanner thought, and he got queasy to even imagine telling him how he felt. His stomached knotted itself into a monkey's fist. He couldn't decide what to do and was running through the situations in his head and growing ever more nauseous when there was a quiet knock on his bedroom door.

"Come in." Tanner's voice came out quieter than he had intended, getting choked up somewhere in his throat.

Timothy opened the door and walked in. He looked as handsome as ever, Tanner let himself observe. He wore a white button-up shirt atop dark jeans. His breath was quick, and a drop of sweat revealed his nerves as it lingered on his brow. During their period apart, Timothy's features seemed to become more enhanced, his jawline chiseled and his bone structure more pronounced, his appearance matching his entrance into adulthood. Tanner noticed all this and welcomed him in, closing his eyes in anticipation of what could be a friendship ending encounter if not handled correctly.

"Hey, Tan," Timothy said, trying to sound casual but failing. "Thanks for letting me stop by."

"Yeah, well, it's like your second home here anyway, isn't it?" Tanner smiled, trying to show that there were no hard feelings. Boys are terrible at communicating.

"Hey, uh, I know this is wicked awkward, but we should

talk." Timothy turned to face him.

"Yeah, we probably should," Tanner replied. "I'm sorry that everything went down like it did. To be honest with you, I can't even remember why we started fighting."

"Me either. It was stupid, and I shouldn't have let it gone on as long as I did. It's just that I..." He stopped and looked painfully conflicted, unsure of whether or not to continue.

"What?"

"I... I don't know."

"Oh." Tanner nodded and looked down at the floor. In a quiet voice, trying to retain as much masculinity as he could, he continued, "I missed ya."

For a while, Timothy didn't say anything, and the tension was thick. Finally, he looked up.

"Tanner, I have to tell you something." Tanner looked over at him, hope in his eyes. A smile broke his face, but he quickly hid it. He didn't want to get his hopes up, for it was probably nothing. The smile did not go unnoticed. He looked the other way and walked to his desk, pretending to look for something.

"Yeah?" he replied. Still pretending to be occupied at his desk, he turned around to look over at his companion. "What is it?"

Timothy was standing entirely too close. The two were exactly the same height (they always had been), and Timothy was looking right into Tanner's eyes. Tanner's muscles refused to budge, and he had trouble catching his breath. Thankfully, he could almost taste Timothy's breath a few inches away. Mmm... spearmint.

In a throaty whisper, the words dancing on the exhale of air rather than being formed as words themselves, Timothy said, "I missed you too." The world stopped existing, and for a moment in time, it was just the two of them standing inches apart. It could have been a second or a minute or a year later, Tanner wasn't sure, but the distance was closed, and with an explosion of lightning that shot through every muscle and every nerve, erupting out the tips of his fingers and down his legs and into the ground, they kissed.

What seemed to be minutes later, Timothy pulled back and looked Tanner in the eyes.

"I knew it."

"You did?" Tanner asked, confused as to how Timothy could know something he himself had not. He tried to catch his breath. "How?"

"You were always checking me out," he said, raising his eyebrows matter of factly. He swooped in and gave Tanner another peck on the lips and playfully pushed him away, jumping onto his bed. They were intoxicated with relief and happiness, their hearts light in their chests, threatening to beat up and out at any moment.

Hours later, Tanner held Timothy in his arms as the two lay on the bed and looked up at the ceiling, silently thinking. Timothy shifted his body so he could better face his mate, and for the first time all night, he looked worried.

"What is it? What's wrong?" Tanner asked, pushing himself back to look at him but not letting go.

"It's just... your dad... my parents... the team." He looked pained. "What are we going to do, Tan?"

Tanner paused, then pulled him close.

"I don't know." He held his lover tightly. "But I promise it will be okay."

That night they existed as one, connected. The light shining from Tanner's attic bedroom cheerfully extinguished, a flash amongst the many blinking lights of the town. Each light turning on or off represented the continuation and progress of a community, a step forward in time. On the southside,

Laura Augustine flicked on the light to her vanity mirror where she was removing her makeup after a wonderful first date with Gavin Prior, who had just turned on his headlights after driving home from the florist, where he arranged for a bouquet to be sent to Laura the next day.

Down the hall from Laura, Mary Augustine contributed to the light show, turning off her lamp after a night of tedious paperwork. She had been applying for the English Education department at the University of Masschusetts, finally having found a program she could be passionate about. She no longer was thinking about George Rutherford, having learned what she could from the situation and moved on to working toward a better life she knew she was capable of.

George sat alone in front of the harsh blue glow of his television, the light unchanging, a DVD being watched for the ninth time. He wasn't aware that in a few short hours, he would be greeting Drug Enforcement Agents at his front door – the same agents who had learned of his activities from Elijah Hart, who taken a deal to save his business and his family. They had held him and questioned him, expecting those lower down on the totem pole of the drug business would be more inclined to talk, especially when threatened with jailtime.

By and by, however, Ipswich was improving on the whole, emerging into the summer as a better community. Each flicker of light was caused by someone who had thrown their problems to the side and taken control of their own lives. They discovered the priceless lesson that happiness didn't just fall from the sky, but rather a decision had to be made to work for its achievement. Not a fate, but a choice. All they needed was a little push. Such is life.

PART FIVE

Now are frolic; not a mouse
Shall disturb this hallow'd house:
I am sent with broom before
To sweep the dust behind the door

V.ii.17-20 *A Midsummer Night's Dream*, William Shakespeare

Perran

Using her master key, Tabetha Ramsay gained access to the school after hours, desperately searching for a book she required over the summer break but had forgotten on one of the bookshelves in her classroom. She searched only by the light of the moon, filtering in through the wavy antique glass. It was a clear summer night.

Her long red hair, lacking its normal frizziness, fell halfway down her back, and she wore a sundress with a floral print. Even without makeup, she looked quite beautiful as she pushed the spines of the used novels and plays into a tight bunch, searching for the small leather bound book that lay forgotten somewhere amongst them. It was completely silent, and the door was locked behind her, only the rustling of paper making a soft background noise as she was left to her own thoughts.

Somehow, she wasn't surprised when she looked up and saw Perran Nemerov standing in the middle of the classroom, shirtless and shoeless like he preferred, the glistening tattoos scrawled across his chest, reflecting the moonlight like no other tattoos could. When she looked up, he smiled his timeless smile.

"I wanted to see you last, Tabetha," he said, hands at his side. She smiled back.

"How kind." She stood up from the short bookshelf she was examining. "So, you've finished then?"

"I did what needed to be done. Although not perfect, it was one of my better efforts, I believe. I stayed fairly uninvolved." He smirked in spite of himself.

"Oh, Perran, I saw a look in Gavin Prior's eyes months back that suggested you were quite involved," she said, tilting her head in kind accusation.

"That was temporary. I lifted my influence shortly after their first date, and he is just as interested as ever. Like I always say, I do not create a false reality. I simply identify the potential and give people—"

"—a push in the right direction," she finished for him. "Just like you did with me so many years ago."

"You were a beautiful eight-year-old, Tabetha Ramsay."

Sixty years had passed.

"And what of the others? Tanner Prior?"

"He has accepted his truth. He was difficult. I had to earn his respect before he would let me in, and when he did, he didn't like what I had to say. He knew it to be true, though, and accepted it in the end. Barber was ready from the beginning, just hesitant. They are happy now."

Tabetha smiled at the good news. "I saw that coming many years ago, and I thought to myself how fortunate Prior would be if you were around. Imagine my surprise when I saw your name on my roster last summer."

"I assume it was quite a shock. I was surprised myself when I first arrived. I'm not sure if you know the fellow, but I was quite stunned to see George Rutherford in town. I had helped him while he was living in New York with a job opportunity that would have led him to success. I'm not sure what happened, though I was saddened to see him here, especially leading young Mary Augustine on when I was working to bring her to a state of self-confidence. I think things will work out for her. She barely needed a nudge. About George, well, I'm not as optimistic."

"You can't win them all." She gave him a comforting look, even though she knew he didn't need it. She still thought of him as a boy, a childhood companion.

"Indeed," he continued, leaning on one of the desks. "I was worried I would lose Laura Augustine to her own self-pity as well. I had to arrange for her ex-husband to return and remind her why she deserved better. Coming across his address in the book I nabbed from her daughter helped wonderfully to influence that. Their meeting turned ugly, but she needed that to move on. She will be happy with Gavin, I am sure."

Tabetha considered all this – how Perran went from one

community to another, whether as small as Ipswich or as big as New York, using his charm and mystical influence to help people rise to their potential. He was a needed push to close the gap in a race, a hand to pull you back from the ledge after your balance was irrevocably lost. He was a relic of hope and the knowledge that happiness is a choice, not a fate, timeless and ageless, much like Perran himself. She wondered what could have been if not for him. As long as time flowed forward, he drifted into the lives of thousands like a rogue leaf on the wind, brushing against many on his way through the world.

"It truly was a pleasure to see you, Tabetha. You have grown into a beautiful human being and could not have made me more proud." The window of the third-story classroom silently opened, letting in the gentle summer night breeze. He stepped to the ledge, bathed in moonlight. "Perhaps in another life, our paths will cross again." And with a final smile and wink of his piercing blue eyes, he stepped from ledge and disappeared into the endless void that was the night, a blank canvas and fresh start, leading to whatever the dawn may bring. Tabetha smiled as the night washed over her face.

"Perhaps."

NOTE ON THE AUTHOR

Alexander DeLuca lives between Boston, Massachusetts and New York City and is pursuing the limitless possibilities of higher education at Northeastern University. He is currently hard at work on his second novel. Meanwhile, he juggles school, work, and solving the world's problems before he reaches thirty.

NOTE ON PRODUCTION

These pages are set in Adobe Garamond, size 11, and were published by the wonderful people at MediaCake. Printing and Distribution were managed by the team at Lightning Source, Inc., an Ingram Book Company. The cover art and interior text were designed and formatted by Alexander DeLuca, and the author's portrait was taken by Amin Roozitalab.

www.AlexDeLuca.com
www.AminRoozitalab.com

NOTE ON THE SETTING

This story takes place in a fictional town with fictional inhabitants. Though there is a real Ipswich, Massachusetts, this is not it. If, however, you are interested in the town described on the pages of this novel, it is based on a very real place. Newburyport, Massachusetts is located northeast of Ipswich along the North Shore, right below New Hampshire on the mouth of the Merrimack River. There, you will find the businesses that influenced those mentioned in the story (albeit under different names) as well as downtown and the boardwalk. The Prior home can be found on High Street in the suburbs of the southside near I-95. Notably absent from this very real town is Saint Andrews, but one look at the local public high school, and you will see the beautiful architecture that influenced the description of the fictional private academy. For more information, including accomodations and events, visit www.cityofnewburyport.com

BookPlus+ Content

Author Interview
A Conversation with Alexander DeLuca

Growing up in the small New England town off of which Ipswich is based, did you draw on any of your childhood experiences for characters or events in Six Months in Ipswich?

Certainly. New England is often depicted as a picture-perfect Puritan fairy tale. Indeed, when you first visit, it looks like one! The truth is, New England is just like every other part of America. There are drug abuse and distribution, divorce, issues of sexuality, death, and class conflict. I drew the characters of Mike Cassidy and George Rutherford from very personal experiences I had in high school. I had a friend who was a creative soul who lost control of his unhealthy habits, turning to drug distribution and self-destruction as his only escape. He graduated many years ago, but I believe he still lives in his parents' basement apartment. It's odd, because the positive memories I have of him as a person are completely different than the reality he chose for himself. It is a good example of knowing when to cut ties and choosing your own path, much like Mary learned to do. I think it is exactly what the character of Perran stands for – choosing your own happiness.

There were many characters who were entering adulthood in Six Months In Ipswich. Did you put any of your own personal growth during that time period into any of your characters?

I can say with confidence that I put a little bit of myself into every character in the book, in a certain capacity. It's mentioned that Timothy is into theater, which was one of my passions growing up. Additionally, I know very well the nerve wracking process of coming out in high school, so Tanner's story was one that was very close to my heart, even if I wasn't a soccer star. Mary's beginnings are an echo of a period of my life where I was lost in my worlds of fantasy. I read books nonstop and made fan websites for my favorite series during the awkward transitions into high school. I don't think I was comfortable with the person I was at the time, and I used the fantasy books as an escape to another world where I wasn't forced to face any truths and could simply revel in the magic presented to me. I still read a great deal, but I balance it with many other things in my life that are important, like schoolwork, running, and of course, friends and family.

You moved around a lot growing up before ending up in New England. How does it differ in culture from other parts of America?

New England is like no other place I've ever been. It can be simultaneously open minded and puritanical, liberal and close minded, and all others sorts of contradictory qualities. What I love about it, though, is that no matter what, people in New England have an ability to shed their differences, much like Laura and Gavin closing the gaps between the northside and southside, and appreciate each other as fellow members of a community. People may argue in town hall meetings for hours on end about the dimensions of a new sidewalk, but in the end, everyone is a neighbor and a family member, and I find that in New England it's easy to remember that. There is also a certain pride that comes from living in the birthplace of America. The surroundings and history that you experience simply walking down the street are like nothing I've experienced anywhere else.

What was your writing process like for the creation of Six Months in Ipswich?

After the initial character sketches and outline that determined what Six Months In Ipswich would be, the bulk of the writing happened very rapidly. I believe it took just under sixteen days to get the first draft of the manuscript completed, which was the result of a challenge to myself to complete it in under a month. The story flowed very naturally; there was only a brief period when I was unsure of what would happen. About halfway through my third or fourth character sketch, the story revealed itself to me, as if it had always been waiting to be told. As my first completed novel, this was an odd sensation. Though the first part went very quickly, the rest of the process was drawn out. Revising and editing took up more time than the actual writing of the first draft! It taught me a lot about the fiction writing process and quickily dissolved any misguided views of the writing profession that I previously had held.

Six Months In Ipswich is your first published novel. Have you been working on other books as well? What can we expect from you?

Before I wrote Six Months In Ipswich, I had a fairly large portion of an epic fantasy novel completed but decided to shelf it indefinitely. I don't know if it will ever see the light of day, but it's possible. In the more immediate future, however, I'm currently working on my next modern-day fiction with the working title The Inherent Beauty of a Grid. It's story about a young teacher suffering from obsessive-compulsive disorder who is sent on an adventure across America. After Inherent Beauty is complete, I plan to finish a memoir and am currently brainstorming ideas for a humorous novel as well. Additionally, I will continue to update my blog, Writing Without Supervision, and have received a great deal of support from the loyal readers during the creation of Six Months In Ipswich, for which I am very grateful.

Readers' Guide

A Reader's Discussion Guide to Six Month In Ipswich

We hope the following questions will stimulate discussion for reading groups and provide a deeper understanding of Six Months in Ipswich for every reader.

1. When George lets himself give in to temptations and chooses a life of destructive decisions, Mary has thankfully matured enough to know when to cut away and leave him in the past. How is this an important time for Mary's development, not only for growing her confidence but as an adult in general?

2. In the press release for Six Months in Ipswich, author Alexander DeLuca mentions that while the protagonist of the story is immortal, it is not a fantasy novel. It is often described as "a character driven portrait of modern New England and its problems that are hidden behind closed doors." How are the elements of the novel both dramatic and commonplace? Which characters leap out of the page and into reality for you, and why?

3. At the conclusion of the novel, the narrator comments on what the town has learned, saying "Each flicker of light representing a person or family that had been apathetic and stuck, going nowhere fast. But these same people had realized the power of hope. They discovered the priceless lesson that happiness didn't just fall from the sky, but rather a decision had to be made to work for its achievement. Not a fate, but a choice. All they needed was a little push." How do you apply this philosophy on making your own happiness in everyday life?

4. What motifs do you see repeated throughout Six Months in Ipswich? The title suggests the timing of the story is of importance. Could the melting of the New England winter into spring and summer represent the awakening of the five residents who are slowly warming to life changing decisions they must make? Besides weather, what other symbolism do you find in the story?

5. Though it seems that throughout Six Months in Ipswich, there is class conflict and separation between the wealthy and

the working class, Laura and George look beyond it and connect. Have you ever encountered a community where such a separation was so apparent? Were you forced to cross the gap for one reason or another, and what was the result?

6. Six Months in Ipswich is a look into the problems of a modern New England town that are often shielded from the public eye. Do you think the issues such as drug abuse, divorce, alcoholism, coming out of the closet, burying feelings from the loss of a loved one to tragedy, and escaping too often to a fantasy world are common in your town? How are they addressed in your experiences?

7. Angela's Diner mentioned in Six Months In Ipswich was a place where people from all different backgrounds came together and shed their differences. They could all enjoy the restaurant as one community rather than the different groupings they otherwise were divided into. What places or businesses near you do you know of that have similar qualities of community and unity?

8. Tanner finally comes to terms with his sexuality in Part Four of Six Months in Ipswich, in the eyes of the reader. There are hints, however, that he knew what was going on much earlier. When do you think he knew the truth about his feelings for Timothy, regardless of whether he allowed himself to admit it or not?

9. Did you find Mary's confidence to shed herself of the destructive George at the conclusion of Six Months In Ipswich

surprising? Contrast her actions at the end of the novel to her personality in the beginning. How did she grow? What were the most influential events to her growth? Do you think she would have gone down the same path had Perran not found Ipswich?

10. Tabetha Ramsay both opens and closes the story of Six Months in Ipswich. Through her several conversations with Perran, we get the impression that she has seen him more than once since he left her in the park at the beginning of the novel. What evidence is there that Tabetha helped conspire with Perran to help fix the problems that were plaguing the citizens of Ipswich? Do you think Perran was involved with more residents than those mentioned in the book?

ACKNOWLEDGMENTS

Many people came together to assist in the creation of this book. Oftentimes, people imagine a lonely writer typing away at their desk, and many months and cups of coffee later, a finished manuscript is sent to the presses. The truth of the matter is that a book (this being my first, hence learning many of these lessons the hard way) is a collaborative effort. Many people assisted with ideas, editing, style, flow, or simply inspired me to use a trait or appearance for a character. Some are simply important people in my life that merit mentioning, having helped me mature into the person I am today, indirectly making this story possible. Those people are the following.

Todd DeLuca, for being a great editor and an even greater dad.

Colleen DeLuca, for being nothing at all like Laura Augustine and giving me the perfect childhood.

Meghan Keady, for inspiring traits in several characters and reminding us all that Phoebes do exist in the world.

Eldon Thompson, for his continued support and priceless writing advice.

Nick Rencricca, for inspiring sections of the story and opening my mind to things I am unsure I would have learned without him.

Tom Gustafson and Cory James Krueckeberg, for creating the movie Were the World Mine that similarly inspired this story and was a guilty pleasure during the events that kickstarted the completion of the first draft.

Dr. Hank Venuti, for showing me the layers of literature I never knew existed, opening my mind to the true artform of the crafted English language, and for forcing me to read and enjoy James Joyce's Dubliners at a time in my life when I would have considered such a feat impossible.

Sandy Elkin, for teaching me to dance in an English class. We miss you still, Mrs. Elkin.

Dave Eggers, for giving me inspiration with his unparalleled talent.

Terry Goodkind, for writing the Sword of Truth series that I grew up with, inspiring some of the many values that Perran stands for.

J.K. Rowling, for the obvious reasons.

The dedicated staff of Georgetown Middle / High School, who, despite my bias, provide a great education and the most welcoming and accepting atmosphere within any public school system I have ever encountered.

The city of Newburyport for providing the picturesque backdrop for this story.

Zachary Hill-Whilton, for giving me a reason to start writing this story.

Christina Grappi, for implanting visions and hopes of summertime cross-country roadtrips, bohemian loft apartments, and ironed grilled cheeses that keep me going when the day is long and my head is aching.

Ron Gilbert, for emailing me back when I sent a childhood fan letter regarding his creations, making me feel like even I could create something some day.

Jimmy Beggan, for continued kindness and support when I need it most, even when I don't deserve it.

Barry Ann Alonzo and Amanda Girard, who, when combined, inspired a character that I wish had more time in the spotlight.

Brennon Slattery, for his continued support and expert plot and style advice.

And of course, all my family and friends who will hate me for not being mentioned by name but are by no means less important. The book would double in size if I included you all, which would cost a lot, so be sure that your contributions and support are noted and held dearly in my heart.

Exclusive Content Password

615332390

Redeem at **media**cake.com